PRAISE FOR STIGMA:

"The author brings to light an important part of New York history, the arrival of the first Jewish immigrants, Sephardic Jews of Iberian origins."

(Chico Neto, Jornal de Brasilia)

"With vibrant realism, Valdívia writes with the tenacity of someone seeking to relate the sacred."

(Leon Frejda Szklarowsky, Vice-President – Consulex Magazine)

"Communicating history through fiction is a challenge, but Valdívia Beauchamp accomplishes that task in this book."

(Carol Almeida, Jornal do Comêrcio, Recife)

"Telling the story of Sephardic Jews in the New World, Beauchamp reveals the age of Dutch America in a mobile perspective."

(Maria Eduarda Antunes, Diário de Pernambuco, Recife)

"Beauchamp narrates the story of the diaspora of 23 Jews who arrived in New York in 1654 in a delightful way."

(Carlos Fernandes, Revista Continente Multicultural)

"A curious history of Sephardic Jews traveling from Portugal and Holland to New Holland and New Amsterdam."

(Jornal do Brasil)

"Using an engenious structure, alternating between fiction and history, present and past, research and fantasy, words and images, Beauchamp, in a successful balance, provokes our imagination."

(Folha de Pernambuco, Recife)

STIGMA

Saga for a New World

For the lucky one on this Christmas Bazaar for Wings, with my best wishes Shalom! Val Beauchamp

New York, December 1st, 2004

STIGMA

Saga for a New World

New York • 2004

STIGMA

Saga for a

New World

Cover – City of Delft – Holland
Bico de Pena Sec. XVII
Stigma – mark made of iron and fire.

Saga of a people who planted their roots in two cities of the New World: Recife and New York.

RB INSTITUTO RICARDO BRENNAND

Valdívia S. Beauchamp

vbeauchamp@nyc.rr.com

Library of Congress Control Number: 2004096245

Published by:
Pacific Cities Press
New York, 2004

Distributed by:
Luso-Brazilian Books
560 West 180th Street, Ste 304 New York, NY 10033
Telephone: (800) 727-LUSO Fax: (212) 568-0147
info@lusobraz.com
www.lusobraz.com

Table of Contents

Dedication

To my parents Francisco Targino de Siqueira and Angélica Lucas de Siqueira. my daughter Angélica, my son-in-law Duane, and my grandson Alan, with love.

Valdívia

Acknowledgments

This book connects me, not only with my roots, but also to those who helped mold my academic growth.

Among many who helped me, I can not forget professors Wilson Martins and Helen Andersen of the Spanish and Portuguese department of New York University, and professors Erdmute White, Enrique Caracciolo Trejo and Paul Dixon from the language department of Purdue University.

Friends and professionals contributed with their kindness, including Caroline Stark, chief librarian of the Queens Borough Public Library, in Rockaway, the late Rabbi Joseph Weiss of Rockaway Synagogue for his infinite Jewish sources, and Yvone Booy, my connection to museums in Holland.

In Brazil, Dr. Jane Coelho Magalhães Melo helped with her vast collection of publications pertinent to the subject. And friends and journalists Raimundo Carrero, Daisy Cisneiros, and Dr. Lino Rocha, helped me put this book in its proper context.

And the professional people at Edições Bagaço in Recife took particularly tender care in the design and publication of this book. They earned their slogan: "To cultivate our culture is our duty."

A WORD OF RECOGNITION:

The wealth of a people is found, in a sense, in its past and its history, and the pages of that history are illuminated still more when they portray spirits who, knowing their origins, preserve the deeds of their forebearers.

The Pernambucan Ricardo Brennand is one of these cyclopedic spirits, whose vast vision and humanist spirit didn't keep his fortune to himself, but instead bequeathed it to future generations.

The São João Castle of the Ricardo Brennand Institute

Mahattan Island, New York, 2001

Introduction

A mis soledades voy, de mis soledades vengo, porque para andar comigo, me bastan mis pensamientos

(Lope de Vega)

I waited a long time before writing this book. I wondered how best to interest the reader in an important history of a people who have contributed so expressively to society in Northeastern Brazil in the 17th century.

At the threshold of a new century, we live in confused and agitated times, in the so-called information age; the values that have formed our character and our culture are being challenged by new, diluting ideas.

But are we obliged to play this risky, virtual game, in which a generation is engaged in pushing the limits of society and erasing the achievements of the past?

At any rate, I have decided, in spite of my reservations, to write this book now. STIGMA, its title, is an ontological mark that includes the imagination and the sensitivity of a generation of people, the dreams and experiences at two geographical sites in the New World, which have not been erased, but have been revived in the spiral of time.

Linking the distant past of the 17th century to the current 21st century, this romance narrative shows the historical, political, economic, and cultural connection that exists between the city of Recife in the Northeast of Brazil and the city of New York in the Northeast of the U.S. This connection is represented by the synagogue Zur Israel in the port section of Recife, and the Shearith Israel in Manhattan, New York. The first was built during the Dutch colonization period under Count Johannes Mauritius van Nassau in Brazil, and the latter under Pieter Stuyvesant in the U.S.

It could easily be argued that this narrative should include the origins of these two cities and how they developed, and the first attempts of the Dutch and the Portuguese Jews to interact with the local natives during that period of colonization. However, I have decided to focus on the life and acts of Count Johannes Mauritius van Nassau as the governor of New Holland (now Recife), the beginning of the saga of the Sephardic Jews in northeastern Brazil. I have also highlighted the economic politics of the West India Company (WIC), which forced Nassau off center stage, thereby losing what today would have been Dutch Brazil. Inserted in this same story is the fleeing of twenty three Jews from Recife, to what at that time was known as New Amsterdam, which changed the cultural and political history of New York.

I also debated revealing epic facts in a romance, but not necessarily in the form of an epic romance. It was then that I realized, that in this sea of events, in the numerous types of information I had collected, there was consensus between my thoughts and my objectives, in the "Saga of the Twenty Three Sephardim," documented by Saul Levi Mortera, which could provide colorful harmony to the development of this book.

After much reading and note taking, I came to understand that in one way or another, the life and values of the Brazilians, the Dutch, the Jews, and also the Americans, who all lived in Recife at that time, contributed greatly in establishing the economy of both cities, although it remained under the control of the WIC and was also affected by the pirating corsairs and adventurers on the Atlantic Ocean between Africa, Brazil, and North America.

Another important part of this story is that at the time when the New World was being discovered and colonized, the politics of persecution of the Holy Office and the pressure of the decadent Holy Roman Germanic Empire did everything to try to maintain the hegemony of the Church in the world, however, the new manners of thinking and conduct barred its efforts and tyranny. Even so, scores of heroes and heroines still preserve in their minds and hearts the stigma of their ancestors' suffering and faith.

If the reader comes to understand the historic and emotional perspective that is presented in STIGMA, I will have achieved my goal.

Chapter – Meeting

Manufacturing Sugar

After the sugar cane is harvested and the leaves are washed away, it is cut in palm length size. Then it is pressed so that the juice flows into a copper container. It is then diluted with water and boiled for a specified number of hours, while the foam is continuously scooped off the top. When the water has evaporated, what remains is poured into clay pots-molds-shaped like cones or pyramids and is left to crystallize. The holes in these molds, which at first are kept closed, to keep the sugar moist, are then opened to allow the syrup to flow out, purifying the sugar. Then the molds are covered, because it is believed that by repeating this sequence several times the impurities are more thoroughly removed, and the sugar becomes lighter in color. This is the first time he addresses this subject.

(Gaspar Barleu, em 1647)

"I've seen this book," Sarah thought to herself as she read a few sentences from the book that was on display in the exhibition "The Dutch in Brazil from 1624 to 2003," at the National Museum of the American Indian, in downtown Manhattan, New York.

At that moment, she became aware of the presence of a stranger, who was looking over her right shoulder, apparently also trying to read the title of the book.

They had both been diligently taking notes on all of the paintings on display. Gaining courage, he turned to her and asked, "What is it that makes New York still feel so upside down a year after the September 11 attacks? Doesn't it make you nervous to be in the city? The security is so tight around here."

Sarah glanced at him, annoyed, "Just a second."

She turned back to the paintings of Albert Eckhout, examining them intently.

Jacob, becoming impatient, repeated his question, "Aren't you frightened to live in New York?"

"No," she said. "I keep myself busy as a journalist. And I'm careful about whom I talk to and what's going on around me."

"What you mean is that you're cautious."

"You could say that," she answered. "But, I try not to get caught up in the hysteria that seems to be everywhere."

"And what do you think about that?" he said.

"About what?"

"About all these people, these crowds that come to exhibitions like this in New York, especially in this part of town?"

"I understand what you're saying," she replied. "This is a big crowd, isn't it? I can see how it might be frightening."

"Sure, this area in Battery Park is too close to all the confusion in Manhattan. There are tourists going on pilgrimages to Ground Zero, and there's a lot of paranoia from September 11, 2001 affecting everything."

There was still some suspicion in her voice as she continued, "I'm curious to know what your notes say about these paintings of Eckhout? By the way, I'm Sarah Drewisch. I'm Brazilian; my father is Dutch and my Mother's Brazilian. I grew up in Delft, southern Holland, and Recife, in Pernambuco, Brazil. I already had the chance to see the book we were reading in the other room."

"You mean *Cultura e Opulência do Brasil?*" he asked.

"Yes, I skimmed through it at the Museu do Açúcar in Recife, a few years ago, it's incredibly interesting, and I can't help wondering how the Instituto Ricardo Brennand came to mount such a wonderful traveling exhibition here in New York on Brazilian culture from the era of Count Johannes Mauritius van Nassau, who influenced the culture in northeastern Brazil so greatly.

"How interesting!" he exclaimed. "What a coincidence! I'm Jacob, and I'm of Dutch descent too, and to answer your question, I try to keep up with anthropology. I'm interested in the sciences, sociology, and anthropology of various cultures like: the African, the Pre-Colombian, and especially the Brazilian culture that's on display here today. Like you, I'm a student of history, and I'm always trying to learn more. Can you tell me anything about the *engenhos*, the sugar cane plantations and the mills?"

Manor House at the Engenho Camaragibe, 17th century

"Yes, my ancestors' *engenho* is still there in Pernambuco, called Engenho Camaragibe. I was curious to see how this exhibit would describe the initial distribution and leasing of land and the industrial and commercial activities of the 17th century. These measures produced the foundation for the Brazilian economy, which attracted the interest of the *senhores*, the landowners, from Holland. And it's really too bad that even today, with all the modernization that has occurred, the relationship between the *senhores de engenho* and their workers in the field haven't really changed much."

Jacob listened contentedly while they walked around the exhibition. As they passed one of the displays, they stopped in front of another very old book, this one dated 1625, *El Brasil Restituido,* by Lope Felix de Vega Carpio (1562-1635), known as Lope de Vega, when Jacob softly whispered:

> *A mis soledades voy, de mis soledades vengo, porque para andar comigo, mi bastan mis pensamientos.*

She smiled as she listened to him. She remembered having heard this verse before. This moment of reflection left her mind fuzzy, as if she were facing a puzzle.

Ricardo Brennand Institute –
Aerial view of the Castle

Jacob couldn't contain his curiosity either. He wanted to learn how he could get to know her better.

"Jacob, if you knew the *Instituto* or had gone to Recife in 2002 for the opening of the Eckhout exhibit, you'd have a better idea of what we're seeing. The preparation for this *vernissage* must have been incredible. And this time, they also included paintings by other artists of the period like Frans Post. What they've been able to do here is fantastic, Jacob."

"Did you see that exhibit in Recife," he asked.

"No, my Mother sent me all the information about the exhibit. She was one of five thousand people invited to the event. In Recife, the exhibit had the atmosphere of an extravagant event that we are accustomed to. In New York, things are done differently. Early New Yorkers didn't have a tradition of royalty, or even a fixed government structure, and as a consequence, I think, they are more casual; they avoided some of the snobbishness and arrogance that we grew up with."

Jacob watched her, and said, "Last year I went to an exhibit of maritime instruments at Fort Tilden. I loved it. The installation was fantastic. You could see very early ships and navigational instruments from the times of the explorers. There were also a lot of paintings from the 15th, 16th and 17th centuries. The show was beautifully curated. The works from those centuries were pristine and the explanation texts really clear. It was also a traveling exhibition sponsored by the

Embassy of Portugal. To tell you the truth, it reminded me of Expo 98 in Lisbon."

"I saw that maritime exhibit too," she said. "Do you realize they chose the perfect location for an exhibition about the Dutch colonization of New Amsterdam, which is now, of course, New York."

"What do you mean?"

"Fort Tilden in Riis Park in Rockaway Beach is the historical site going back to the time of the Dutch arrival in New York, in 1625," she said. "They even built windmills in the area, to remind them of their homeland."

"Riis Park?" she added, "was the name given in honor of Jacob Riis, a commander of the local army under Stuyvesant, at this fort, during the expansion of the government in the 17th century. It was in Rockaway that the Dutch started to spread out, with their ports and piers, building New Amsterdam. The old maps are incredibly interesting. You can see exactly what they did with the areas of land between Jamaica Bay, the East River, the Hudson River, and the waterways."

She continued, "The story of the Dutch in those times really intrigues me, Jacob. Their knowledge on how to turn flooded land areas into usable land was their trademark in New York as well as in Recife."

"You know so much about this, I'd love to talk more about it after the exhibit," Jacob said as he was walking around the room.

They continued examining and reading sections of the 17th and 18th century books, commenting to each other, and laughing at the customs of the times, until they came to a panel highlighting a definition for *senhor de engenho*:

O ser Senhor de Engenho, he título, a que muitos aspiraõ; porque traz consigo o ser servido, obedecido, & respeitado de muitos. E se for, qual deve ser, homem de cabedal, & governo; bem se pode estimar no Brasil o ser Senhor de Engenho, quanto proporcionadamente se estimaõ os Títulos entre os Fidalgos do Reyno.

Many aspire to the title of Senhor de Engenho, because it signifies to be served and obeyed, respected by many. And if he is, as he should be, a man of wisdom, governor; one can imagine what it means to be Senhor de Engenho in Brazil, based on the extent that titles are valued by the noblemen of the kingdom.

(in Antonil, Cultura e Opulencia do Brasil, Lisboa, 1711, ed.fac-símile. See translation in margin.)

"What an interesting idea, Jacob. The title of Fidalgos do Reyno or noblemen of the kingdom meant that everything was under their command."

ENGENHO PERNAMBUCO – Engraving by Frans Post, *Praefectura Peranambuca, pars Boreaealis*, published in the book by Barleu, 1647.

They continued enjoying the paintings, with the crowd slowly moving, until they stopped in front of one by Frans Post entitled *Paisagem com plantação (o Engenho)*, from 1668.

"How beautiful."

"Oh yes. This is still in the times of the engenhos, Jacob. Look on this side of one of the two rivers that divide the city Recife (the Capibaribe River) and observe who is working on the riverbank in Pernambuco."

"Just a second, Sarah, I want to read this." He was focusing on the Museu Boijmas van Beuningen in Rotterdam, and then asked, "How many of them are slaves?"

"The *senhores de engenho* couldn't do the work by themselves," she replied. "They depended on the 'workforce.' If an engenho stopped producing sugar, the losses would be enormous: the sugar cane that had been harvested would go to waste, and the *senhor de engenho* would then owe the government, actually the West India Company (WIC), even more. It seems like history is repeating itself still...."

"Would you know how much it would have cost to lease land back then?"

"Historians say that in Count Johannes Mauritius van Nassau's day, it cost 7.5 million florins. Because of the huge amount involved, he tried to find aide for the *senhores de engenho*, to avoid what would be catastrophic losses for the WIC."

"He must have been under a tremendous amount of pressure," Jacob said.

"Right. Read this, and you'll understand it a little bit better."

Convém proceder com brandura em relação aos lavradores e aos senhores de engenho, antevendo assim a revolta que começa a fermentar no âmbito da indústria do açúcar.

> *It is best to proceed with caution as to the planters and senhores de engenho, thus being proactive concerning the dissatisfaction that is beginning to ferment in the sugar.*
>
> (Testamento Político do Conde de Nassau, *1644.*
> *See translation in margin.)*

"Those twenty four years that the Dutch governed Brazil weren't easy. We learn this in elementary school. It was one war or battle after another, mostly because the Dutch didn't get along with the Indians, nor with the Blacks, making it difficult, after their conquests, to be accepted by the locals, much less to become their allies."

"Sarah, I'd like to know more about this part of the history of Pernambuco and how it ended up affecting things here in New York. It seems to me that

TAPUIA INDIAN – Oil on canvas, Albert Eckhout, 1641 – National Museum of Denmark.

the *senhores de engenho* did, after all, form an uprising that brought down the WIC."

"You're right, but the socioeconomic structure in Pernambuco, especially in the rural areas, is pretty much the same today. Back then, the *senhores* maintained a feudal system, where there were uprisings and many deaths related to the parcels of land for lease; today the socially excluded, the 'landless,' are still trying to find their place within the same structure."

"That's terrible, but still, I'd like to go to Brazil to see an actual *engenho*."

They stood in front of one of the paintings by Albert Eckhout, Mulher Tupi, 1641. Sarah looked at the wall text commentary.

"Look at this. In the background you can see the casa-grande (manor house) of an *engenho*. I saw some Eckhout paintings in Europe too and found out that he had gone with Count Johannes Mauritius van Nassau to Brazil when he was 26 years old."

Listen, I'll read it aloud: "Eckhout became renowned as one of the first to portray ethnographically the richness of the people at that time"

"You have to admit," Sarah added, "that miscegenation did not begin with the colonial occupation, but it was to them a natural consequence of their circumstances. The mazombos, the Brazilian natives, as they were called by the Dutch, came to have a style all their own."

Let me continue reading: "We see this in the next painting. Note, the common result of miscegenation. Here, Eckhout paints *A Mulher Tupi* (1641), a cross between a native Indian and a white person. The Tapuias were a feral, even man-hating tribe."

They looked at the painting of a wild Tapuia Indian, who carries on her back a basket containing fruit and a human foot, and in her right hand she holds part of an arm and a human hand.

"Cannibalism!" he exclaimed.

"Yes, however, in the days of Count Johannes Mauritius van Nassau, everything looked different to European eyes. The New Continent was a mysterious place, more exotic, and it was a place to make a fortune. So much so, that when he arrived with his large advisory committee, the Count built the Palacio de Friburgo (Vrijburg) Boa Vista (1643), the first observatory of the Americas (where the first solar eclipse was registered in November, 1640 by the cartographer and astronomer Georg Marcgrave, and even a Calvinist Temple (1642). He improved streets and developed urban sanitation, organized a large garden with fruit trees and medicinal plants, and set up the first zoo of the Americas with animals from the region and from Africa. He was the greatest entrepreneur to appear in a long time.

"The architectural plants and designs came from Holland, ordered by him. Nassau brought with him, for example, one of the best architects of his time, Pieter Post, brother of landscape painter Frans Post, who always accompanied Nassau on his voyages into conquered lands, and who managed to produce 160 works.

"Who came before Nassau, Sarah?"

"It was Sir Diederik van Waerdenbuch, who later affirmed out of jealousy that he was not of noble descent, nor, as we know, did anything for northeastern Brazil, either."

"Can you go a little further? What was Mauricio van Nassau really like?"

"A prince, the son of the Count John VII and his second wife, Margarida von Holstein-Sonderburg. He was born on June 17, 1604, in Dilemburgo, Germany. He pursued a military career, achieving the rank of Colonel, and after several victories in battles, was invited by the Council of the Nineteen of the West India Company to head the civil and military government of Dutch Brazil. He lived in Brazil from 1637 to 1644, arriving and departing in the same ship, the Zurphen. He loved Brazil, was called 'the Brazilian' by the locals, and took with him many native objects from Pernambuco (including a hammock), upon his return to his homeland."

MAURITIUS VAN NASSAU – Oil on canvas, work by Johannes de Baen, 1665, Mauritshuis, The Hague.

"What a great history lesson. And, how old was he when he arrived in Recife?"

"Thirty-three," she replied. "Now, take a look at his portrait right there beside you. See, Johannes Mauritius van Nassau–Siegen."

For a few minutes they looked at his noble pose, at the painting by Johannes de Baen, of the prince in military dress.

"He looks like Salvador Dali, with that big moustache," Jacob joked.

"No, are you kidding? Look at the way he carried himself, even though we're only seeing part of his torso."

"It's interesting to me, dear Sarah, that there have always been conquests and wars and crusades that were used to gain social power in the world. The same

The resistance to the economic and cultural imperialism of the countries in the west, especially the United States, took the form of religious fundamentalism, because the countries affected by this imperialism did not have any other cultural means to mobilize. It is unfortunate (many Arabs and Muslims continue doing this) that the resistance to the domination and imperialism did not find means other than the most traditional and archaic religious tradition. But it should not be forgotten that the economic and social structures of the colonial or neocolonial domination contributued to the perpetration, and were not intended to favor any modernization of the religious message....

(Interview of Pierre Bourdieu by the jornalist Luciano Trigo, in Continente, *nº 14, Feb. 2002, Recife.)*

is happening again now with another kind of battle, the holy war. Centuries ago, the crusaders were intent on spreading Christianity, at least that's what they claimed. And in this current war, it is becoming clear that the fundamentalist Muslims with their jihad are intent on destroying the so-called Jewish-Christian civilization."

"And what it is that we learn from war?" she asked. "The Christians may say the anti-Christ has been found, but to the Jews there is another connotation."

"I don't know," he replied. "All I know is that this time, both the Jews and the Americans are being persecuted by these religious fundamentalists."

"I agree with what Pierre Bourdieu says," she answered. "He says that the problem continues to be a lack of cultural alternatives for the peoples in the Middle East."

"I have read some of his works, too. Do you want to stop and get something to eat?"

"Sure," she replied. "Would you like to sit down awhile, maybe in the coffee shop? Do you have time? Are you hungry?"

"Yes. I took a few hours off today. You know, we've been walking around, looking at the exhibition for over two hours now. — Do you know if it's downstairs or upstairs?"

"It's right over there, Jacob, at the end of the ground floor. Can you see it?"

"Where? Oh, I see it. I see the long line, too."

"Don't worry. This line always moves fast—it's self-serve."

"What would you like to eat? I'll get it."

"I don't know. Maybe a tuna sandwich and some orange juice."

"I'll have the same."

"Good," he said. "Please find a table while I get in line."

From her vantage point at the table, Sarah watched Jacob. He seemed intelligent, elegant, and pleasant. The eating place was crowded which caused, in her, an atmosphere of anxiety common since the attacks on the World Trade Center towers. Sarah wanted to talk about the pre-Colombian culture, which she felt confident discussing, but she wasn't looking for a relationship.

Sarah had been living in New York for a number of years. She was working at a local newspaper and was familiar with New York life, having moved there when she was young. She completed her studies at New York University Graduate School of Arts and Sciences, with a degree in journalism. She understood city life, especially from the point of view of women in the city, the majority of whom chose to live alone, as she did. For her, in this context, single men knew they were at a disadvantage, and they felt sorry for themselves in this "Single's City," what they derogatorily called the Big Apple.

She also knew that she and many other women, single by choice, would only make a serious commitment if they could have it all. The amount of time that a career woman, like herself, had to be either at the newspaper editor's desk or traveling on business, was too little to keep up with the basic needs of a family, that is, the cooking and cleaning, not to mention the financial and social obligations.

Sarah, now in her 50s, was levelheaded, a widow with an only son living in Paris—she constantly traveled to see him. Paris was her first love, she had gone there many times on vacation as a child living in Holland with her parents.

From where she was, she could see Jacob, and she waved at him as he walked towards her with the tray of food.

"I brought you some soup, too," he announced.

"Thanks, but I don't know if I can eat that much."

"It's cream of asparagus soup," he countered, "and it will be great with the sandwich."

"Mmm!" she said. "It's delicious. Great choice. By the way, did you happen to see how they heated it? Was it in the microwave?"

"Yes, why?" he asked. "Are you afraid of radiation?"

"A little," she replied. "I'm just aware of things like that."

"Sarah?" he said, changing the subject, "I'd like to know more about the plantations of Dutch Brazil."

"Well, where should I start?" she said. "In the process of acquiring the mills that had been burned at the beginning of the Batavian occupation, the WIC established its own policies for rural credit. The *senhores de engenho* were responsible for an understanding of what were acquiring, such as the choice of sites for the sugar cane fields and the pastures, and where the water was located. Upon receiving the lands, they had to pledge loyalty to the Count and also commit to the ethics involved with the leasing of lands to the *lavradores*, workers at the *engenhos*, as explained by Antonil, later in the 18th century.

Feita a compra, não falte a seu tempo a palavra que deu, pague e seja pontual nesta parte...(evitando)...demandas e pleitos, que são uma contínua desinquietação da Alma e um contínuo sangrador de rio de dinheiro, que vai a entrar nas casas dos advogados, Solicitadores e Escrivães, com pouco proveito de quem promove o pleito, ainda quando alcança, depois de tantos gostos e desgostos, em seu favor, a sentença.

> *After the purchase, do not be delinquent on your word that you gave, pay and be timely... (avoiding) ... demands and lawsuits, which cause a continuous unrest of the Soul and a continuous bleeding of rivers of money, that enter the houses of the lawyers, Creditors and Notaries, with little advantage for the person who is moving the lawsuit, even if he achieves, after much success and grief, a favorable sentence.*
>
> *(op.cit. See translation in margin.)*

"Do you think the history of economic catastrophe is the cause of the country's rebellions?" he asked.

"I think it was like a pervasive bankruptcy. The Portuguese, Brazilians and many other newcomers had debts not only to the WIC, but also to the private creditors among the outstanding business people in the colony, Dutch capitalists, and Sephardic Jews. The *senhores de engenho*, however, were the cause of this financial ruin; they earmarked a good part of the income for city expenses or they sent it to their homelands in Europe. On the one hand, the *senhor de engenho*, who controlled sugar production, needed not only the labor of the slaves, but also that of the immigrants who were constantly arriving from Holland. On the other hand, his carelessness in business and his authoritarian and violent conduct in harvesting the sugar cane, gave rise

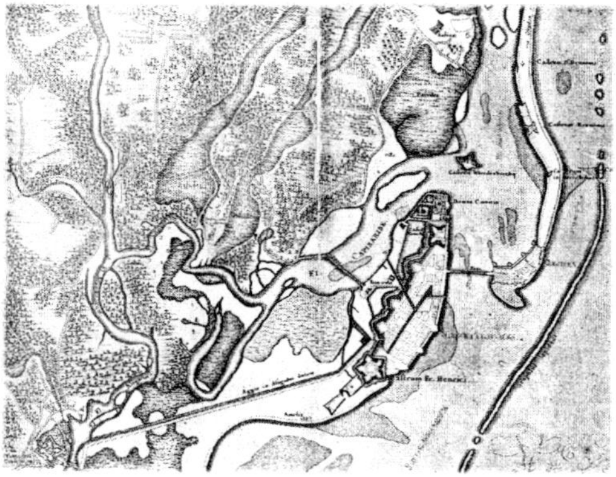

CIDADE MAURICIA – Engraving of Mauritiopolis Reciffa, published in the work of Barleus.

to mysterious fires being set, slaves running away, and especially the neglect of the sugar cane workers, who didn't adapt to this situation and migrated to urban areas. For those arriving from Holland, going to the city of Mauricia also provided them with something else: an environment very similar to what they were used to—lots of water, canals, bridges, and proximity to the sea. The Africans, though, went into the forests and set up their quilombos. As, the sugar cane harvest decreased, the production of sugar weakened, and business slowed. The heads of the WIC, however, refused to accept this situation."

"Wait a minute, please," he interrupted. "Are we going to talk about the positive side of the story? There are numerous good things; for instance, the Count turned Recife into a metropolis. He started to clear out the slum areas where the immigrants were living, in the port area, and paved and provided sanitation for the streets."

"Have you seen any records from that time?" she asked.

"Sure," he said. "Gaspar Schmalkalden, for example, who Nassau brought over with him, left various maps showing the areas that were filled in so the city could be expanded, and also kept a diary."

"Jacob, when we get back to the exhibit, I'll show you an important detail that you missed."

"What is that?"

"I'm talking about the reference to the various religions in Recife, which had not been so visible when it was a Portuguese colony. There were of course privileges for some and restrictions for others: the Calvinists received more privileges, but neither the Catholics nor the Jews were allowed to have public gatherings (the former were permitted to have their services only in their homes; the latter were authorized to build a synagogue, which was, actually, the first one in the New World, and was named Kahal Kadosh Zur Israel, which as you know means The Holy Community of the Rock of Israel. According to the historians, Nassau also had a vision of peaceful religious coexistence."

"One more addendum." she continued, "Among the Catholic *senhores de engenho*, on the day of the botada (first day of the sugar cane pressing), the priest of the *engenho* was called to bless the moenda, press, and the tools used in producing the sugar. It was a day of celebration for everyone at the *engenho*."

"That's wonderful. I'm delighted by everything you're saying. I've also studied a little about the Dutch conquests, readings I had to do for my PhD dissertation, which was entitled 'A parallel between the dominion of the trade of specialty goods in the 16th and 17th centuries and the control of oil production today.' Of course my analyses were always based on political and economical aspects. You said your mother is Brazilian, right? I did a lot of research about Pernambuco, and especially Recife, for my dissertation. Where is she from?"

"She's actually from Recife, Pernambuco."

"That's another coincidence," Jacob said. "I've heard stories about the Dutch since I was little. Before I went to college, I lived in Brooklyn with my parents, Orthodox Marranos, who retold the stories about the Dutch conquests in Brazil, the Caribbean, and especially the expansion of New Amsterdam in 1625."

"So then you probably heard about the works of Jan Andres Moerbeck, a Dutchman who lived in

Freedom of conscience is not freedom to practice religion, a fact alluded to by Count van Nassau in advising the Council of the XIX: there is a greater need to practice tolerance and condescendence in Brazil than at any other place where people have been given freedom of religion.

(Leonardo Dantas Silva, in Continente-Documento, *Cepe, 2002, p.13.)*

Olinda, Pernambuco in 1624 and wrote about Brazil, marking the beginning of the Dutch attacks. Yes, I grew up hearing these stories too."

"What do you think of these books, Sarah?"

"Wow! These are old! This one was from 1647. Let me see if I can read the title: *Rerum per octennium in Brasilia et alibi nuper gestarum sub pr fectura Illustrissimi Comitis J. Mauritii, Nassovi, c. Comitis, nuc Vesali Gubernatoris Equitatus Federatorum Belgii Ordd. Sub Auriaco Ductoris historia*, written by Caspar Barleus."

They read it silently, and suddenly they spoke at the same time, "That's a complicated title," laughing.

"Although there's a translation of it here in the exhibition text," he said: "History of the recent endeavors undertaken during eight years in Brazil."

The book was displayed open on a bookshelf with the following: To the very illustrious Count Johannes Mauritius van Nassau, Ex- Governor of Dutch Brazil, etc.:

> *I hereby offer you, Illustrious Count, Brazil, aggrandized by your authority and by your arms. If this country could speak and make a treaty with you, it would lay itself at your feet, you, who with great valor have defended and exalted Holland, and filled Spain with the fame and fear of the other, which are both in awe of you. That which neither one nor the other can, I will do for one and the other, by recording history so that the acts performed and the performer of the acts will not be forgotten. The old historians, who transmitted for posterity facts dignified to be handed down over the centuries, did not pass on the terms of the Old World. We dare to seek with you*

Aqui vos ofereço, ilustríssimo Conde, o Brasil engrandecido pela vossa autoridade e pelas vossas armas. Se ele pudesse falar e firmar convosco um tratado, por si mesmo se entregaria a vós, que, com insigne galhardia, defendestes e exaltastes a Holanda e enchestes a Espanha com a fama e o temor da outra e o assombro de ambas.

O que nem esta nem aquela podem fazer, fá-lo-ei por uma e outra, escrevendo uma história na qual nem serão esquecidos os feitos praticados, nem omitido o autor deles. Os escritores antigos que transmitiram à posteridade fatos dignos de atravessar os séculos não transpuseram os termos do velho mundo. Nós, audazes, buscamos convosco um mundo que, apartado de nossas plagas por um oceano inteiro, parece ter a natureza guardado e escondido para honra vossa e glória da casa de Nassau...

> *a world, on the other side of an entire ocean, which appears to have saved and hidden its nature for your honor, and the glory of the House of Nassau...*
>
> ***(Translation by C. Brandão, ed. USP/Itatiaia, BH, 1974. See translation in margin.)***

"It's very interesting for one important reason: although the author is openly incomplete, in the presentation and analysis of facts, it is a book with an enormous variety of current information, in general collected from those who actually experienced it. It was ordered by the main party interested in it, Nassau, as recorded by Cláudio Brandão, the translator, recalling the words of Frei Rafael de Jesus:

Escreveo & pintou, & pintou em tudo que escreveo.

> *He wrote and he painted; and he painted in whatever he wrote.*

"Now this one here, Jacob: *Cultura e Opulência do Brasil por suas Drogas e Minas*, published several years later, in 1710, was written by a Jesuit who, they say, hid behind a pseudonym, André João Antonil. This book was banned for quite some time by "El Rei" based on the argument that it would disclose the specific locations of the riches in Brazil...."

Jacob was quite impressed by all that Sarah was telling him. He had never seen a sugar mill, nor had he known about some of the peculiarities as to how slavery had developed in Brazil and its association with a type of feudalism that had its origins in the Hereditary Captaincies.

Jacob murmured again:

The citation by Lope de Veja, "A mis soledades vengo..." refers to the Sephardic Jews, who like nomads were isolated and lived unto themselves, accompanied only by their thoughts.

> *A mis soledades voy, de mis soledades vengo, porque para andar comigo, mi bastam mis pensamientos.*

Of all the books on display, the one that most caught Jacob's attention was the *Diário de um Soldado da Companhia das Índias Ocidentais*, 1629-1632, by Richshoffer. It was a simple diary, written by a soldier enlisted by the Dutch army. He wrote extensively about Recife and Olinda."

Olinda at that time was considered the wealthiest city in Portuguese America," Sarah said. "But the bourgeois of the city, when they saw the Dutch arriving, set fire to their own *engenhos*, destroying everything, causing losses to the WIC never before seen. It was at this point that the decision was made to expand the city of Recife, the so-called *Aldeia do Porto* by the Dutch. Logistics favored a flatter land for a port. There the entire community of the *engenhos* would converge downtown to attend mass, Special Saints Days, Te Deum, and Novenas at the Church of the Corpo Santo or at the Convento de Santo Antônio, where the elite in Pernambuco usually gathered, according to Frei Manoel Calado who wrote Valoroso Lucideno. The Catholics received permission to celebrate mass in their homes behind closed doors, but they could not have processions for the festivals of saints. The Jews built their synagogue on the Rua dos Judeus, and were also restricted to practicing their rituals behind closed

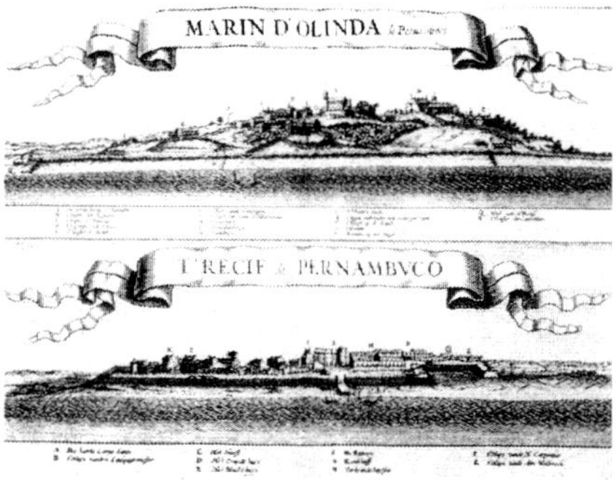

MAPS OF OLINDA AND PERNAMBUCO – Engraving from the book History or Annals of the Achievements of the Privileged West India Company, by Ioannis de Laet, Leiden, 1644.

doors," Sarah continued. "Another tradition was having garden parties around the manor houses where the Mucamas and the Blacks, according to custom, would dress in silk clothes with large collars similar to the European style, and serve tropical fruit juices, squeezed by hand, in vases made of agate and sardonyx, which were actual murrinos (Barleus). While at the same time, accompanying and caring for the children."

After a big pause, Jacob said, "Some of the objects in my apartment look like that."

"Objects?" Sarah asked, "Are they worth a lot? Are they authentic?"

"They're articles made of feathers: headdresses, necklaces made of coconuts, etc., from centuries ago."

And laughing, he ended the conversation leaving her question in the air.

"This is all very interesting, Jacob, but we need to hurry. I still need to go to the office today."

"Wait. You can't leave without seeing the rest of the paintings. Look at this one right in front of us by Frans Post: *Paisagem brasileira com nativos dançando e capela* (no date). It is a very special one, look at the faithful walking towards the chapel at the *engenho*, their families all dressed up in their Sunday best, and in the background the slaves singing and dancing with their drums. In the distance there is low vegetation, hills, and a lot of water."

"I can imagine how much activity there must have been at that time, with the huge numbers of soldiers and sailors arriving at the port," she added. "I also read about the time of New Amsterdam, the situation there generated by these immigrants created problems for the government practically impossible to solve. Even the Protestant Calvinist pastors couldn't

RELIGIOUS SYNCRETISM – Oil on wood. Frans Post. Brazilian landscape, slaves dancing in front of a church, showing thus the beginning of various forms of religious manifestations (XVII century).

get their followers to go to church once every week. The objective was to provide moral standards for the members of the community, who preferred to spend their time in the lodges and bars that were opening."

"I can imagine there had to be a lot of problems. We know that the areas where the immigrants lived in Recife, before the arrival of Nassau, were considered "pigpens," the worst of slums, with a large number of men living in the same house. After Nassau arrived he started to work on Recife to make it more like a city, until the Cidade Maurícia was planned."

"I can just see everyone rushing around," said Jacob, "trying to build their houses, dealing with building sanitation, paved streets, an urban place, instead of rustic sleeping quarters."

"Since you haven't let me leave," she said laughing, "let's take a look at this other painting by Eckhout, 'Mandioca.' For seven years, he documented all the fauna and flora in the region, trying to show that it was possible to cultivate these plants. When he returned to Holland with the same advisory committee of Nassau, he had produced twenty four paintings, of which twelve were still-life, all the same size (90 x 90cm)."

"There is a very interesting reference to manioc cultivation (which he describes as Miscellanea cleyeri), in which the Count, knowing manioc's nutritional value, made it mandatory for all the land workers to grow this root in their yards—it had to be a part of their meals either cooked or fried, or made into flour or starch. This is why he commanded his soldiers to supervise the plantations."

"Certain foods were given a lot of importance at that time."

"Right," Sarah answered, "including green coconuts—coconut water became so popular that it influenced the Scotch palate; in Pernambuco, whisky is served with ice cubes made of coconut water and is considered a very exotic delicacy."

"What about this exotic Black woman in front of us?"

"The title of the painting is *Negra com o menino* (1634-1641), Eckhout. This painting, as I recall reading in Recife's exhibit catalogue, raised a lot of discussion, because it was compared to *Mulher negra*, by Tierbuch de Zacharias Wagener, a German explorer who said that the individuals born of the Blacks and the Portuguese were called *Mulatos*, and were to be considered slaves, condemned to spending the rest of their lives in captivity (in Eckhout *Volta ao Brasil*, 1644-2002). Nevertheless, the painting itself is beautiful. The basket that she carries with fruit and flowers, was said to have been one of two baskets, collection of the Kunstkammer Real da Dinamarca, which belonged to the scientist and collector Ole Worm. It was discovered after his death (1654) in the 1674 inventory, that American Indians commonly carried two baskets.

"Jacob, the Nassau era was a high point for Pernambuco. His committee of advisors was considered one of the best, and for that reason fostered even more feudalism in the government. The *senhores de engenho*, who were mostly Jews, were wealthy and bought their slaves, branding them on their foreheads or their chests with their monograms. The Dutch also had their *engenhos*, the Blacks that they owned to run their moendas and ovens. They acquired them in auctions. For their protection the WIC provided bows and arrows, shields, swords, huge clubs of hardwood, and other

MAMELUCA WITH BASKET – Detail of oil on Canvas, Albert Eckhout, 1641, Royal Museum of Denmark

weapons, according to *Diário de um Soldado*, trying to help them against the almost daily skirmishes with their enemies in their immediate surroundings. The soldiers, however, would go to battle with their pockets full of gunpowder, bullets, and fuses."

"Jacob," she continued, "in order to understand the culture that resulted from the great miscegenation that began in the Portuguese colonies, especially in the Captaincy of Pernambuco, you have to know the etymology of the word, Pernambuco, which was very well explained by Barleus: 'an opening that the natives called in their language, a rock with a hole in it that made the sea that forms the throat of the arrecifes (reefs).' Then you will be able to understand better why Recife was chosen to be the port city, and so on."

"Little by little, Sarah, I can visualize it; it's very clear that this place was like the land in Holland, which is actually why the Dutch put so much effort into filling in the land, building bridges, literally investing in a land similar to their homeland."

"Yet, about the etymology of the word Pernambuco. The word *Parana* = para - na is translated as 'similar to the sea,' in other words, *lagamar*, which in this case is formed by the joining of the Rio Capibaribe and the Rio Beberibe, by the hole, the opening, and the outcropping of the rock, says Barleus. That's why the final explanation revolves around the margins of the two rivers and the sea. The Count definitely tried to implant his culture in the conquered land. He held horse riding tournaments between the Northern Europeans and the Portuguese noblemen or the Brazilians from the region (Gilberto Freyre, *Sobrados e Mucambos*), where the riders were distinguished by their mounting style, or rather, 'The animals that were ridden side straddle by the Northern Dutch... did not have the graceful riding style of the Portuguese, who rode sitting forward and tight in the saddles." (Recorded by G. Freyre in *Sobrados e Mucambos*, according to an observation made by the priest and historian Frei Manual dos Óculos, page 147).

Suddenly she looked at her watch, "Jacob, I have to go."

"Will I see you again, Sarah? May I call you? I'm really interested in learning more about Recife."

"Of course," she said, as they exchanged cards.

His read:

Jacob Spinoza
Prof. of Anthropology
Columbia University

Hers read:

Sarah Herckmann
Reporter
The Day

Jacob was very handsome—tall, dark hair, and brown eyes. He was a Professor at Columbia University where he taught Anthropology. He was also active in one of the local museums and member of a committee at the American Museum of Natural History between 81st St. and Central Park West. Since he had started his Masters Program at Columbia University, he had moved from Brooklyn to Riverside Park, at the corner of 90th street, to a small studio apartment. It was nice—a convenient place for him to live—near the university and centrally located. He had easily developed a love for the place. The view of the Hudson River was beautiful and relaxing, with boats sailing past the Palisades on the other side of the Hudson. But what was more important to him was that from his small apartment he could keep an eye on the marina on his side of the Hudson River, where his fifty foot long boat was anchored.

Jacob really knew how to make the most of his surroundings. He jogged daily and exercised on the boardwalk with the other amateur athletes, and in the afternoons, he rode his bicycle to the university. His boat was his favorite toy. He liked to take his guests fishing or just for pleasant rides around the island. He was a typical bachelor, and he had his own idiosyncrasies and habits, but he was not Orthodox in the Judaism in which he was raised.

Born in Borrow Park, he frequented two yeshivas and had been well educated. His favorite synagogue was the Shearith Israel, founded at the time of New Amsterdam (XVII century), through which various Rabbis passed who lived in Europe.

The Marranos, from the time of his great, great, great-grandparents, as well as the Ashkenazim, had attended this synagogue.

Jacob was a descendent of Spinoza. His great, great, great-grandparents had arrived in America in the 17th century and came to Ellis Island, through which all immigrants passed. Luckily, his family remained in New York. His great, great, great-grandfather had an apothecary in Europe, and upon their arrival

SPINOZA – Baruch, Bento or Benedictus Espinoza (Spinoza), 1632-1677, was born in Amsterdam, the son of Spanish and Portuguese Jews. He was probably a student of Manasseh ben Israel. He was excommunicated in 1656 for opposing orthodoxy. He did not renounce Judaism and his criticisms of fundamental religious principles were refuted by Jacob de Andrade Velosino, born in Recife, in a work written in Portuguese.

in New York they were soon called on to help out in the community. The demand in this area was tremendous.

They were able to have their business and residence in the same building in New York. It was a relatively nice house, on 57th St. in Brooklyn. It is still there today, with nuances of a Dutch-style home, a relic of New Amsterdam. It was his great, great, great-grandfather on his Father's side who was a direct descendent of the Portuguese philosopher Baruch Spinoza. Philosophy had been a main topic of discussion in his family. His great-grandfather had also been a professor at Columbia University; however, he did not have a reputation like Spinosa. He published various essays on ethics.

He had married a Dutch Jewish girl, was comfortable with his Semitism, and sometimes shied away from more polemic themes related to the life of his famous relative. Jacob was also raised in a very closed community, consisting only of Orthodox Jews, but was the one who least fit in, perhaps because he had the genes of Baruch Spinoza!

Even though he had various interests, he had never considered studying to be a Rabbi, as one of his brothers had (his younger brother was a medical doctor). Nevertheless, he always observed all of the Jewish holidays.

At this moment in particular, his presence was frequently requested by his family to discuss the possibility of moving away from New York, although they didn't know where they would go. "It's okay," he would say, "we are Sephardim." And that was his answer every time the discussion about moving hit a snag.

Chapter – The 1950s

Sarah had turned into a beautiful, attractive, and some might say, sensual woman. She was born in Recife and had lived there a few years when she was very young. The rest of her childhood and teen years had been spent in Recife, Delft, Amsterdam, and The Hague.

As a child, she fit the stereotype of a little Dutch girl. On Sundays or holidays, when she went to the Recife Country Club with her parents, or played with her little friends, she stood out because her features were so Nordic. She was pretty, well educated, a bit of a snob, but she always treated adults respectfully, calling her parents' friends "Sir" and "Ma'am," though she kept a certain distance between herself and those who were not family. Anyone who tried to get close to her would feel a wall of ice. It was an innate reaction, probably inherited from her Dutch ancestors. Her entire family was likewise reserved.

In those days, friends of the family knew that her father, Professor Isaacq Drewisch, proudly descended from Dutch nobility. He never removed from his finger the Lapis Lazuli ring with the family crest: a lion surrounded by other characters. Among friends, he would joke about his title and call himself an "ex-Count."

The "ex-Count" was loved and well respected in the society of Recife in the 20th century. He used his openness with the people to take advantage of opportunities that came his way in the community.

Sarah was well cared for by her nursemaids, who raised her in the traditional orthodox manner of a family belonging to a certain elite class that existed in Holland before the First World War.

When she was in Recife, her starched linen dresses, trimmed in bilro lace, with a white apron practically covering her skirt, made her look graceful and even more Dutch. She wore a small scarf and the traditional huik which covered her hair so that only her two blonde shoulder-length braids appeared.

Contrary to what is assumed, the current documents and witnesses show there were a great number of Dutch married to "mulher da terra" or Portuguese girls. Dona. Anna Paes, after the death of her first husband, Charles de Tourlon, married Gisbert de Witt...Counselor of Justice. The Dag Notule of April 29, 1645 states that de Witt informed the High Counsel of his intentions to marry Dona Ana, saying that "his future wife had already shown favoritism to our nation over that of the Portuguese, even during his former marriage."

(Gonsalves de Mello/Jose in Tempo dos Flamengos *– Ediç. do Gov. de Pernambuco – SEC, Dept. de Cultura, Recife 1978, p.144.)*

Sarah was a healthy, happy, and energetic child, with a very light complexion, rosy cheeks, light-colored eyes, hefty legs, and strong wrists and ankles. She was always full of life and curious about everything.

In discussions with her father, she would not let him finish a sentence until he explained everything that she did not understand. Everything she saw or read was an object of inquiry. However, there was one thing which she did not understand yet, because she was so young—the importance of the cultural baggage she was carrying, the family traditions that were the sum of her life.

She had not really known, for example, much about the Sephardim living in Brazil since the 15th century, nor that her mother was a descendent of Dona Branca Dias, who, with all of her descendents, various other New Jews and non-Jews, Portuguese and Dutch women, managed to live together harmoniously during the Catholic Inquisition in Recife.

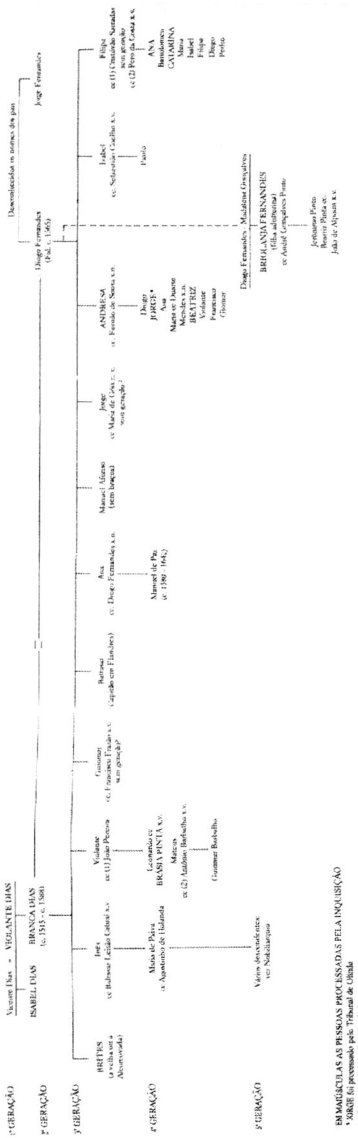

BRANCA DIAS: FOUR GENERATIONS OF THE INQUISITION

One of them was Dona Ana Paes d'Altro, a fearless woman considered to be ahead of her time.

In the annals of Holland, Portugal, Brazil, and the United States, Dona Branca Dias is registered along with her husband Diogo Fernandes, who was a New Christian and traveled to the new continent. In Pernambuco, he received a sesmaria of the lands of Camaragibe, donated by Duarte Coelho, in 1542. Her mother, the daughter of a Jewish woman, had always been against her marrying Diogo Fernandes and was arrested during the Inquisition and denounced Branca along with her son-in-law, affirming that she had received Christian baptism, but converted to Judaism and had stopped practicing the Catholic faith. She performed and obeyed Jewish rituals and ceremonies, for example, placing one more candle in the candelabrum for Shalat, when she put on clean clothes and put clean sheets on her bed. As a family they celebrated the Rosh Hashanah (Jewish New Year), Yom Kippur (Day of Atonement, and the three pilgrimage festivals: Sukkoth (Tents), Pesach (Easter), and Shavuoth (Weeks) on the Jewish calendar. She realized during her interrogation that if she did not confess, her sentence would be more severe—burning at the stake, perhaps. So she admitted their adherence to Jewish practices and was sentenced, in 1544, to two years in jail and to using the penitential habit. A year later, alleging that her husband was far away in Portugal and that she had children to raise, she was released, and returned, apparently, to her home in Viana da Foz do Lima. From there she was able to leave for Brazil where she joined her husband and her eleven children. She passed away between 1579 and 1581.

Curiously, during the visit of the Holy Office to Pernambuco in 1593, Branca Dias, who was already

ARMS OF THE HOUSE OF ORANGE

deceased, was once more denounced to the Inquisition, this time by some of her former embroidery and lace-making students. The accusations were the usual: practicing Jewish customs, this time with additional accusations that she and her husband had come from Portugal banished by the Inquisition, according to Antonio Gonsalves de Mello in *Gente da Nação.*

In Recife, the two-story home of the Drewisch family had been built over the foundation of another that had been there in 1644, according to archeological research carried out in the area, when the building was being remodeled and the structure reinforced. Today there is talk of declaring it a Historic Landmark, because it may be a historical mark from the Flemish period.

After Count Mauritius van Nassau arrived in January of 1637 and the Flemish conquest had been consolidated, the issue of housing became a priority for the government.

The old capital had been destroyed,

> *what was still of use from the demolished city's rubble was transported to Recife to be used in new construction, so that although the mother—Olinda—had disappeared, from the ruins would arise, with a different countenance, her daughter—Mauriciople.*
>
> **(Barleus,** ***ed.USP/Liv.Itatiaia, BH, 1974, p. 154)***

Transportou cada um para o Recife os restos e os entulhos vendíveis da cidade demolida, aproveitando os materiais em novas edificações para que, desaparecendo a mãe – Olinda –, lhe sobrevivesse das ruínas, embora com outro aspecto, a sua filha – Mauriciópole.

(Barleus, ***ed.USP/Liv. Itatiaia,, BH, 1974, p. 154)***

Fearing that the old capital would be taken over by the Portuguese and the Brazilians and possibly become a concentration of rebellion in the future, the Dutch determined that "anyone wanting to build, will build on the Antonio Vaz Island." On September 12, 1641, the rebuilding of Olinda was officially prohibited.

A bridge connecting the isthmus where the port of Recife was, to the Antonio Vaz Island, the Stad Mauritia, (now the Mauricia or Mauritzstadt), and another connecting the Palácio Boa Vista to the continent, would solve the space problem for housing. This would also alleviate the problem of transporting the sugar to the port by wooden rafts, which depended on the tides, and always entailed losses by the time it was loaded onto the ships. The sugar could now be transported by land in carts.

The Dutch occupation brought about the urbanization of Recife, and later, with the arrival of Nassau, also that of the Antonio Vaz island.

During the time of Count Mauritius van Nassau in Recife, there was intense collaboration between the Portuguese and the Dutch. Gaspar Barleus even stated that:

> *It would be of comfort to the plantation owners and the Portuguese burdened by their debts, if the Company would grant them an extension of time to rebuild their patrimony.*

Seria conforto para os senhores de engenho e para os portugueses esgotados de dívidas, conceder-lhes a Companhia alguma folga de tempo para refazerem o patrimônio.

With this cooperation, residents made daily requests to buy and sell land. Requests were analyzed and were usually negotiated for a hefty amount of florins. Thus, large numbers of Brabantines arrived in Recife, and the urban problems at that time became more and more serious.

Even now, some of these issues remain, which were long ago taken to the Policy Council (1630-1636), the High Secret Council (1637-1646), and the Supreme Government (1647-1654).

When Mauritius van Nassau arrived, the era of Recife architecture flourished. It was a time of great transformations, and social structures began to align themselves. Newcomers arrived and tried to associate themselves with the Count, who made flexible alliances that were constantly modified. The Count, on numerous occasions, befriended the Brazilians and the Portuguese, even joining them in celebrating enthusiastically, in 1641, the acclamation of Dom John IV, as reported in *O Valeroso Lucideno* by Frei Manoel Calado.

There was also widespread construction taking place. Many of the current two-story buildings in Recife were built over the foundations of the structures from that time. Bridges were built: Ponte Velha, Ponte da Boa Vista, including Ponte Mauricio de Nassau, over the Capibaribe River, which connects the residential areas of Santo Antonio to the Recife Districts.

The land auctions during the 17th century constantly subdivided the land into smaller lots. The flow of the immigrants increased daily, and the population in the city of Recife itself already consisted of thousands of inhabitants. Everyone arriving from Holland wanted to build their home as quickly as possible. One of the most popular areas rested along the banks of the Capibaribe

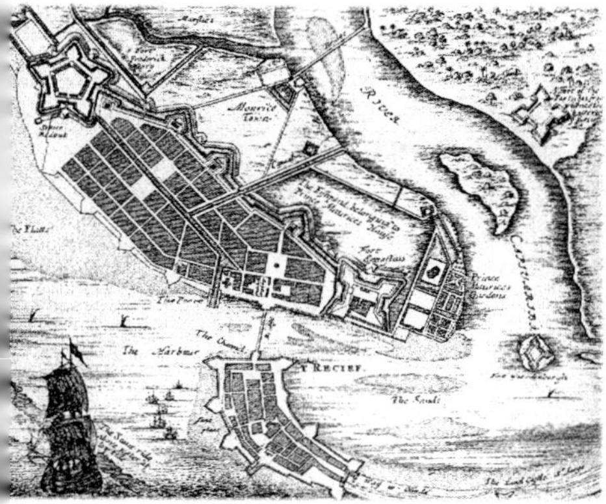

CIDADE MAURÍCIA – Map of Recife, published in the book of Johan Nienhof, London, 1703.

and Beberibe Rivers. The Brabantines tried to transfer to Recife their "urban environment," their modus vivendi from Holland, to the Brazilian Venice, an expression used later in the 18th century, when Bernardo Vieira de Melo, in a patriotic speech reassuming the Chamber of Olinda after the War of the Mascates, compared Recife to Venice in Italy: "Since we are separated from Portugal, let us make our land a republic similar to that of Venice." Actually, this declaration of freedom, according to Mario Sette in *Terras Pernambucanas*, is today considered the first declaration of the Republic in Brazilian lands, by a Brazilian. The regime imposed by the Dutch who occupied northeastern Brazil in the 17th century was in fact the Republic of the Seven United Provinces (also called the Utrecht Union) installed under the leadership of Prince William of Orange-Nassau, in 1579.

Different types of problems were common in the government at that time. During the time of Mauritius, these issues and polemic affairs were never ending and were always reported or recorded by the *schipper*, the person in charge of sending all the correspondence to the directors of the WIC in Holland. It should be mentioned that even though some of the information was reported very quickly—*met der haest Gedaen*—when it was written, just before the ships left, it was very accurate, according to J. Gonsalves de Mello, after reading the *Dagelijksche Notulen der Hooge Raden in Brazilie*, a book on the "Atas do Alto Conselho do Brasil, 1635/1654."

MAP 03 – Illustration of the report of Claes Janszoon Visscher on the conquest of Olinda, 1630.

In 1950, the Drewisch family lived in a two-story home in Apipucos. There were two entryways, one facing the Capibaribe River and the other the Apipucos Reservoir.

A beautiful place, there were various rooms, including an attic, done in a Dutch architectural style common to those times. The windows were framed with a layer of heavy stones. The entire house was built out of bricks, some of which, now weathered by time, may have been produced at the brickyard of Mr. de Witt, the husband of Dona Ana Paes (owner of the Casa Forte sugar mill).

The house was tall and had a slanted roof, which made it possible to collect rain water in agate or clay containers. The architecture was attractive and comfortable, with various windows on the four sides of the house.

The kitchen was towards the back of the house: there was a wood-burning stove in one of the corners and a hardwood table for eight people in another. It had a unique entryway. One had to go down two large steps to get to the kitchen. This would give the impression that the place was actually on a lower floor, making it unattractive.

The family members would not linger very long there; little Sarah was the only one who sometimes remained awhile to lick the pan used to make guava sweet, one of her favorites.

MONOGRAM – Engraving reproduced in the book "Zeeuwen en de Westindische Compagnie," by Doeke Roos.

They usually had breakfast in the patio behind the house, where her father, the professor, caught up on all the news in the newspapers, everyday, before going to work. Other meals were served in the dining room, more or less in the middle section of the house, with a lot of doors opening into it, providing fresh air to the room, which had a beautiful view overlooking the river that flowed around the house.

It was, however, in the kitchen, where the servants spent the day, from which the most pleasant and delicious aromas came. A dozen or so servants worked, making sweets from tropical fruits (guava sweet in syrup), candied bananas in chocolate, grated coconut candy with and without papaya; they melted brown sugar, made butter, little starch balls for the tapioca, and squeezed fruit to make juice.

They ate in the kitchen. All these people in the room made it look like a human ant colony. The heat was unbearable. The owners of the house couldn't bear to stop by, even to get a glass of water, but the servants didn't seem to mind the suffocating heat. Anyone looking in from the outside would have thought that they would have been baked alive in there. The weather in the city of Recife was not pleasant either, so the servants would bathe in the backyard, in the old stream, the Riacho da Prata, for several hours each day, which sometimes got them into trouble.

The patio was very pleasant: the ground was covered with a layer of bricks, and beyond this was the huge yard full of fruit trees. This was also a famous site. Tradition had it that when the previous house was being built, several centuries ago, Mr. de Witt would often arrive at this very spot to ask about the orders of bricks to be delivered from his brickyard.

It appears that the Dutch government in Pernambuco stimulated the development of brickyards: in letters of June, 1643 and May, 1644, it informed Holland that it was no longer necessary to continue sending bricks... since they are being made here and can be purchased for a lesser price.

(JAGM, in* Tempo dos Flamengos, *op.cit., pág 79)

During the beginning of the Dutch conquest, the bricks were shipped by the WIC. After the establishment of industries, however, during the time that could be called the architectural renaissance in Recife, under the command of Count Nassau, the manufacturing of bricks in Recife became possible because of the great demand and the presence of specialized labor, mainly the overseas brick makers. It was a very profitable business.

Many of the new arrivals were artisans, stonemasons, carpenters, and overseers, who contributed greatly to the tremendous increase in construction during this period. This was the reason many of the Dutch already residing in Recife worked with this particular industry.

As for Counselor de Witt, he began to reflect upon the discontentedness of the Brazilians. Mr. de Witt was Counselor to Mauritius van Nassau until the day he was sent back to Holland for conspiring against him. As Counselor of Justice, he lived reclusively in the Casa Forte, and after marrying Dona Ana Paes, he ran one of the biggest brick making businesses in the region.

He was a very complicated person. Before marrying Dona Ana, he had lived in the residential area of the port of Recife, and his office was near the dock area. A proud man very concerned about maintaining a correct political posture at all times, he was always well informed, keeping up on the news and resolutions in Nederlanden, as well as on issues among the Brabantinos, the Batavos, the Portuguese and New Christians in Pernambuco. He had a very high profile for two reasons: he was married to a Portuguese Brazilian, and he worked for the Count.

One fine day, on December 23, 1645, Mr. de Witt arrived home from work, dismounted from his horse to open the gate to his property, and was kidnapped by a group led by the Indian Felipe Camarão, who was very much against the Dutch occupation.

And it was on that night that Dona Ana Paes feared for her survival. Alone, she found herself having to take over the brickyard. She was already very much afraid of the dissident Dutch. After that night, she had to give many depositions about the occurrence and was taken before the High Secret Council many times, until one day she was able to make it clear that she had not been an accomplice of her husband, convincing them that he was a man that didn't deal with his business matters at home, but only in his office at the port of Recife, and in his native Dutch, therefore, there wasn't anything she knew about the business. All of this occurred shortly after the Count Mauritius van Nassau had returned to his native land. Mr. de Witt was finally released by his enemies. But when he presented himself to the Dutch governors, they decided to banish him from Pernambuco anyway.

In 1640, Portugal gained its independence from the Spanish Crown and the Portuguese began to rebound, and among all the confusion, the Dutch one day surrounded the Engenho da Casa Forte. The owner, Ana Paes, was now considered a suspect. Aware of these new attacks by the Dutch, Fernandes Vieira, now commanding the revolt, and his men readied themselves to fight their enemies; hearing about the attack on the *Engenho*, they decided to go there and fight.

The Dutch, seeing they were surrounded, ordered all of their women prisoners to be set up in the windows of the manor in an attempt to discourage the Brazilians that were attacking them. Even today people talk about how brave those women were; they were ready to die for Pernambuco—they shouted and gestured to the Brazilian troops to continue shooting. The attitude of these women allowed the manor house to be taken in one assault, imprisoning all the Dutch and saving these heroines.

Today this two-story building still maintains its majestic air. It is located at the same pleasant site and has the same appearance from yesteryear. Sarah played among the trees of various colors, bordering the entry lane and the area between the patio and the orchard of her house.

She loved to spend time in that yard, where she sometimes rode her pony Valeroso, which her two nursemaids led around.

Way in the back were the quarters of the servants, who liked working for this family, known for their generosity.

From the other side of the house one could see the marrecos and other water birds in the Apipucos Reservoir. In the back of the yard there was a dock where many times one of the servants had to be reprimanded for taking too much time off work, usually to fish.

There weren't many bedrooms in the manor house, and they were not very airy because of the typical Dutch architecture with many small windows set high up in the walls. Sarah's bedroom was nice though, with two windows facing the Reservoir full of bilro lace curtains and a few pieces of colonial furniture, wisely distributed around the room to hide any defects of construction.

The bed was a tall canopy bed, made of *pau brasil*, a family heirloom from the time of the Dutch. It was placed at an angle in one of the corners and was so heavy it was impossible to move for cleaning purposes.

In 1950, her father, Senhor Drewisch, was transferred once again to Delft in Holland; this was not the first nor the second time he returned there with his family. However, this was the first time Sarah would go to school there.

This time the University of The Hague had invited him. Mr. Isaacq Drewisch was a scholar with a specialty in the History of Brazil.

With this move of the Drewisch family, Sarah would be leaving Brazil for several years. But this liason was smooth, she did not experience cultural shock. As a child, she adjusted easily; and besides, everyone spoke Dutch, which she had learned and spoken at home.

In the New World they say that when Europeans first arrive, they maintain an air of superiority because they speak a language of the "civilized" world; but

HEADQUARTERS OF THE DUTCH WEST INDIES COMPANY (WIC) IN DELFT HOLLAND.

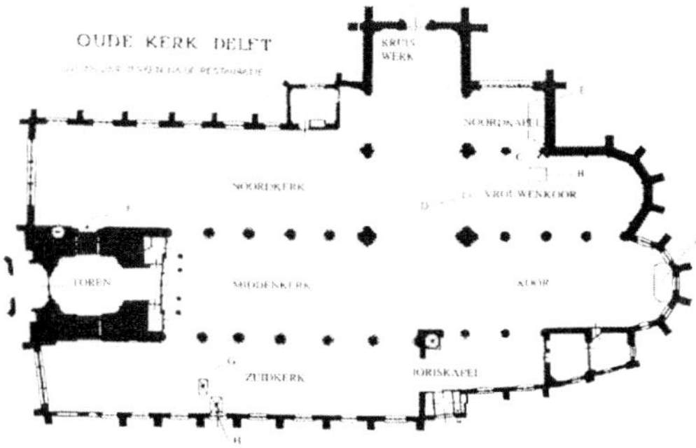

GROUND FLOOR OF THE OLD CHURCH OF DELFT (14TH-15TH CENTURY).

this only lasts until they start to become a part of this irreverent culture, the Brazilian culture. But on the contrary, it was a great experience for Sarah to have spent her adolescence in Delft, where she studied and grew up between Rotterdam, Amsterdam, Harlem, and The Hague. She became acculturated to Europe, feeling comfortable and at home, no longer standing out as a foreigner. She had acquired the local mannerisms and behaviors of a native.

When the family arrived in Delft, following the advice of some of her father's colleagues (a couple, professors at the University of The Hague where he taught), they rented a house on the Rua Lange Geer, one of the most important historical sites in the city of Delft.

Professor Drewisch was very respected among the academia in Brazil as well as in Holland. He made it a point to maintain good relationships with the other staff members of the university and also with the accredited diplomatic corps of the country. At that time, and even a few years after World War II, it was considered a privilege to live in The Hague, where many important international decisions have been and continue to be made.

On the same side of the street where they lived in Delft, two doors down to the right, westward, was one of the most important historical buildings—the office of the WIC, in the 17th century. The residential area was beautiful: on one side of the canal was the

Armentarium, an old arsenal of the Dutch Government from the time of the conquests in the New World. Today, after being largely restored, it has become the Military Museum. On the other side of the canal, across from the museum, was Sarah's house, squeezed in between another, almost identical house, at the end of that street was a wide bridge that led to the port.

The little girl loved to ride her bike along the streets and canals of the city, with her little friends, on days their school, at the synagogue, let out early. They would hop on their bikes and ride around before going home, stopping to buy some candy at the market in front of the Nieuwe Kerk or visit the local museums, which were always changing exhibits.

Sarah had only become interested in Delft, a Medieval city dating back to 1070, after she realized that she lived at a historical site, which she discovered when studying the country's history. She was enthralled when she learned that the city had developed around the castle of the Duke Godfrey de Lorraine, who conquered Holland in the 8th century.

The young girl grew up in a healthy environment. From the beginning, she was taught how important it is to acquire culture and at the same time cultivate freedom while respecting each person's privacy. This philosophy of life created a symbiosis between the Medieval and the present culture, awakening in its inhabitants the desire to keep it alive. Latent also was the Jewish culture that the family exercised freely in Holland, after all the persecution perpetrated by Adolph Hitler.

Her mother was very active in local society. Her father was a member of the Rotary Club and together they participated in philanthropic organizations. Here she made good use of her artistic vein, taking ceramic classes, which alleviated her intense social life she led with her husband.

Once a week, she would go to Rotterdam by train to an art studio that offered classes on the Ceramic of "Royal Delft." Her works were on display in the annex of this studio where there was a folklore room with the students work for sale at a reasonable price. Most of the money she received was donated to local charity institutions, but she always managed to keep for herself ten percent of sales, of course....

It was very enjoyable to look at the rare catalogues with drawings of old ceramic items used since the 15th century. The replicas of old and rare pieces enchanted all the visitors, including the tourists, who would spend hours observing the process of modeling the clay until it reached the ovens. After they were shaped into vases, figures, plates, and tiles and painted in the blue and white "Royal Delft" style of 1653, they were baked until set. Sarah sometimes copied the old pipes and the typical dress of Holland from these ceramics.

Young Sarah was drawn to this type of art also: When she started Middle School, she would often go with her mother to the studio. She loved the short train ride between Delft and Rotterdam; and what was even more fun was that each trip she made, her pipe collection increased.

"Look, Mother, how this pipe is longer than the others."

"Do you think it is for a giant," and teasingly she added, "with big hands? I bet that when the owner of this pipe wanted to smoke, he had to handle the tobacco and that's why it had to be big."

"How do you know that?" the young girl asked, not noticing the teasing tone in her Mother's voice.

"Well, I'll tell you. The navigators in the 16th through 18th centuries were curious about the spices they brought from overseas. They tried to learn from the natives, their skills in using tobacco, herbs, and medicinal drugs. When they learned how to use them, they started to bring them for trade with pharmacies and laboratories in Europe, then giving a good reason for the use of the pipes."

"I have seen several books with drawings of plants from overseas, Mother. Do you know any of them? What are they used for?"

"They're used as medicine. We are familiar with a lot of them, for example Basilicum angelicae, Oculi cancri, Terebinthina, Balsamum copaivae, and others."

"Have you ever given me any of these medicines?"

"No, but your Father likes homeopathic medicines. He's the one who uses them. Have you seen the one he has with the picture of a plant on the label?"

"Yes."

"Well, honey, they're medicinal herbs, not chemicals. As for the size of the pipes, those navigators couldn't understand how the natives from Africa, Asia, and the New World could smoke some of those plants (which they sometimes just rolled up in leaves), so they tried to protect themselves from getting burned. Some of them already understood the medicinal property of these plants as well as their calming properties, but were still concerned there could be other side-effects, and they had their pipes made with very long stems. They had learned from the natives how to roll up a few seeds to smoke then lay down to count the stars, and some perhaps threw them into the sea. That's why these pipes are still found around the docks and the canals of Delft and other cities even now in the 21st century."

Sarah was completely absorbed in her subject, reading a book about ceramic art, Antieke Tegels (old tiles) and trying to copy the picture of a ship from her tile.

The teacher from the studio, hearing the conversation interrupted, adding that when the sailors returned from the New World they also cleaned their ship before they docked at the port, scrubbing the decks, and getting rid of anything that was not really needed to keep the ship clean. And that's why these pipes are found in the seas or in the canals of Delft today, brought in by the tides.

"That's a lot of pipes. I love this little one; I'm going to copy it and take it as a souvenir."

"Do you know what century this one is from?" Sarah asked the teacher.

"Sure, it's a replica of the 16th century; it's beautiful, isn't it? Are you going to copy it?

Sarah led a very healthy life, playing in the brick streets around her city, between the canals of Delft, walking with her little friends up and down the streets, taking piano lessons from a teacher that played in the Symphony Orchestra of Amsterdam. In general her lessons were given at home, her teacher coming twice a week.

Delft – Engraving by Vermeer

Her teacher, Ivone, was very fond of young Sarah. She was a friend of the family and attended the same synagogue in Delft; she was part of the family's close circle of friends. A famous woman, giving piano recitals with the Symphony Orchestra, as well as individual concerts. Her best subject was Mendelssohn, she was a woman of a great sensitivity. Her role in the cultural center of the synagogue was to play the piano for the children's dance classes, religious festivals, and weddings.

In the center of all this, Sarah had a wonderful life. She loved to go to the gatherings at the synagogue where she had the opportunity to meet and socialize with people. On one of these occasions, she had met Professor Van Eckhout, a good friend of her father, and his colleague at the University of Den Haag. A well respected and well known professor in academic circles and society, he was well known for his textbooks, essays and seminars. His most recent book, *Entre holandeses, judeus, portugueses e pernambucanos*, was an essay on the history of the twenty four years of Dutch occupation in Pernambuco, or rather, about the profile of the Dutch rule that occurred in that part of the New World, divided into three distinct periods: 1630 to 1637, 1637 to 1645, and finally 1645 to 1654.

It is important to recall at this point that Prince Mauritius van Nassau himself had finished building his beautiful palace in Den Haag, sending precious wood from Brazil to be used in its construction, and of no lesser value, boxes of sugar, to pay for the expenses. The architect Jacob Van Campos, who along with his brother Frans, a painter, had been part of the nassaoviana committee in the New World, designed this construction. Directors of the WIC maliciously called the palace "suikerpaleis," the "Sugar Palace."

Sarah already knew about this book because her father had recommended it to her in a Saturday meeting at the Cultural Center in the local synagogue on Rua Koomart. The synagogue building dates back to 1862 and is located between the traditional hotel "Leeuwerug," from the 17th century, and a row of look-alike houses in a neoclassic style, facing one of the canals. The synagogue had fought for its space along the canal like the other 8-meter-wide buildings built in accordance to a particular law, since the flourishing of the mercantile republic of that country—the great wealth coming in was applied to the residences of middle class merchants who only bought houses facing the canals.

On this particular day though, Sarah was participating in a group of 13 to 19 year olds in a piano concert which showcased their talents and presented themselves to fine arts managers for future contracts in other European countries.

On that evening, twenty students from music schools in various Dutch cities were participating. It was a beautiful concert, held in the small room at the synagogue reserved for this type of activity. Professor Van Eckhout was among those invited by the family. Sarah was one of the younger recitalists, but executed Mendelssohn's First Concerto, in E Minor, Op. 25, with great ease. After the presentation there was a reception and Prof. Van Eckhout, presented by her father, congratulated her and gave her a copy of his last book. Sarah thanked him and opened it immediately. Reading the title, she turned to Prof. Van Eckhout and told him that she was taking a class in General History so she would certainly be reading the book.

The Professor felt very proud and was already looking forward to the chance to share his knowledge with Sarah. He was an ex-priest and had never had children, and he knew that she was a part of the "story" of his book because of her genetic inheritance—her family had passed through Recife in the early 1600s.

"Mother, this book has information about our family, our ancestors, and how they arrived in Recife in the 16th century."

Her mother right away became interested: "I'd like to read it after you, Sarah."

"I just need to finish my research paper for my History class and then it's all yours, mom."

The young girl really got into the book. Each page contained an interesting issue, like the intricate sugar market between Recife and Holland. At the same time she was discovering more and more about her roots. Whenever she had any questions, she would ask Prof. Van Eckhout about them, and he was more than pleased to help her.

Sarah was very interested in the history of her ancestors, especially their strong influence in her upbringing—her family had raised her in the tradition of nobility. Her father, the "ex-Count," was obsessed about the history of his people, which explained his frequent visits to Holland.

"All right, Sarah, let's step back a little," said the Professor. "The Inquisition was very cruel not only to the Jews, but also to the Protestants and Catholics that were considered heretics."

For example, the approximately 300 families of Sephardic Jews that arrived in Portugal in the 15th century, had been banished from Spain, accused of occupying the social positions that could be filled by the population that was losing its power.

Dissident Calvinists and Protestants lived alongside Catholics and those that had no religion, among a population of about one and a half million people.

In 1543, Charles V, a great persecutor of the faithful, sovereign ruler of Austria, Spain, Borgonha, and other territories in Europe, united all his domains and set up the famous "Seventeen Provinces," which extended from the Baltic Region to the Mediterranean Sea.

When Charles V abdicated in 1555, he left the Kingdom of Spain to his son Philip II, who in turn, reorganized the Inquisition tribunals, previously conducted by his father, to once more persecute the Calvinist Protestants, placing heavy taxation regulations on them.

Later on, however, Prince William, the "Taciturn," backed by the noble rural merchants of the time, became independent from Spain. It was then, in 1579, under his leadership of the "Seven Northern Provinces," that the Utrecht Union was formed. It was only in 1648, with the "Treaty of Westphalia," that the independence of the "Seven Provinces" was recognized, a fact that led to diminishing the power of the Dutch inquisitors.

The backbone of the Dutch Republic in the 17th century following independence from Spain, was made up of free men, free thinkers, like the merchants and navigators, the *cortadores de trufas*, the cheese

JAN VAN OLDENBARNEVELT was born in Amersfoort, Utrecht, on November 25, 1547. He distinguished himself in the war against the Spanish and was "confidente" of Guilherme I, of Orange. Oldenbarnevelt, because of his increasing influence, was called gentleman-at-arms, a title conferred on important government workers. The Prince of Orange, Jan Maurits, an outstanding military official, son of Guilherme I, consolidated the independence of the Low Countries from the Spanish rule, becoming its governor, with the current title Stadhouder. The battle between the Protestants in the North and the Catholics in the South of the Netherlands, led Oldenbarnevelt to sever ties with the Prince, after the peace that had prevailed between England and Spain. With the mediation of France, he ended, in 1609, a 12-year truce that had been respected in Europe and the Spanish possessions. This diplomatic agreement, however, went against the economic interests of the United Provinces. Taking advantage of an internal conflict in the Calvinist Church, the Prince of Orange accused him of heresy, had him imprisoned, and handed him over to a special court, which ordered him to be executed. This occurred in Den Haag, on May 13, 1619. He was head of the civil government of the United Provinces, and he developed trade, founding, in 1602, the West India Company.

manufacturers, the rural agricultural workers, the fishermen in the North Sea, as well as the fishermen on the Rio Reno. This situation offered security in the region, to the political and religious dissidents.

In other words, the provinces at that time acted independently. They would designate a military leader, the *Stadhouder*, who was invariably a member of the House of Orange, or of its ally, the House of Nassau.

After the death of the "Taciturn," in 1584, his son Mauritius van Nassau, was nominated Stadhouder, consolidating the borders of the Republic.

In Holland, the Inquisition was a very serious issue, because the Calvinists defended religious tolerance. They disagreed with the fanatics who wanted at any cost, to banish from the country, the "Papists," Jews, and members of the Protestant sects. At this point, when the great statesman and gentleman-at-arms Jan Van Oldenbarnevelt was head of the government, favoring armistice and desiring to accumulate wealth through trade, he launched the following motto: "In essentials, unity; on questionable issues, freedom; and in everything, charity." And even though this may have been the reason for his demise, it did allow for greater intellectual freedom in Europe, especially in the Dutch Republic.

Rene Descartes spent 30 years in Holland before writing his masterpiece, *Discurso sobre Método*. The philosopher Spinoza, excommunicated by his Jewish brothers, because he did not believe the Old Testament was divinely inspired, praised Amsterdam for the freedom it allowed. In this environment, men of all races and sects lived together harmoniously.

"Was the Stadhouder Nassau the one that built the city Mauricia, which is now Recife?"

"No, Sarah, it was Count Johannes Mauritius van Nassau-Siegen who was also from the Orange dynasty. Later on you will understand all of this."

The Professor continued to explain that way before all of this, the main reasons for the Inquisition date from 1233, when Pope Gregory IX emitted a Papal Bull that conferred to the Dominicans the special task of eradicating heresy in the world, and also established a Permanent Tribunal under the orders of the Dominican Friars. A system was thus created to control people, their ideas, and their thoughts in such a way that if this were today, we would say this was the first Gestapo, the terrible Nazi German Police during Hitler's regime.

The Inquisition later on can be compared to the politics of Stalin, who, in an effort to maintain the Soviet power, killed, persecuted, and exiled whole ethnic groups, moving them from one area to another, from the Urals to Siberia.

Umberto Eco portrayed in his book, *The Name of the Rose*, the methods and techniques used to punish the alleged heretics. There were several, one of the "lightest" being the pilgrimages, described by M. Baigent & R. Leigh:

> *There were two types of pilgrimages. The shorter one implied going on a pilgrimage to 19 Sanctuaries spread out all over France, and at each one the penitente was whipped. The longer pilgrimage involved a long trip—from Languedoc to Santiago de Compostela, to Rome, to Colony, to Cantuária. In the 13th century, penitents were sometimes sent on pilgrimages like Crusades, to the Holy Land, lasting from between two to eight years. If*

Havia duas formas de peregrinação. A menor implicava uma caminhada até dezenove santuários espalhados por toda França, em cada um dos quais o penitente era açoitado. A peregrinação maior envolvia uma longa viagem – do Languedoc a Santiago de Compostela, a Roma, a Colônia, a Cantuária.

No século XIII, penitentes eram às vezes enviados em peregrinação à Terra Santa como cruzados, por alguma coisa entre dois e oito anos. Se sobrevivessem, exigia-se que trouxessem consigo, na volta, uma carta do Patriarca de Jerusalém ou Acre, atestando o seu serviço.

(Baigent & Leigh, in A Inquisição, *Ed.Imago, Rio, 2001, p. 49.)*

para a queima de quatro hereges, a 24 de abril de 1323, as contas de um inquisidor de Carcassonne mostram a seguinte discriminação:
– para lenha grande: 55 sols, 6 deniers;
– para galhos: 21 sols, 3 deniers;
– para palha: 2 sols, 6 deniers;

they survived, they were required to bring with them on their return, a letter from the Patriarch of Jerusalem or Acre, testifying as to their service.

(Baigent & Leigh, in A Inquisição, *Ed.Imago, Rio, 2001, p. 49.)*

Today this type of pilgrimage, for the good of all concerned, has become more of a tourist attraction, although a few still do it out of devotion.

In those days, the heretics were recognized by the way they dressed: a saffron-colored cross sewn on the front and the back of their garments. The goal was to make them repulsive to the general population.

When there was to be an execution, which was usually preceeded by torture before the Inquisitors, there was a procession in front of large crowds, the event having been announced by the reading of proclamations in the four corners of the burg. The condemned person was tied and placed at the top of a tall fire, to be burned, as in the case of Joan of Arc. Yes, it was usually women who received this torture, specifically because they had been found guilty of being witches.

The inquisitors kept thorough records, and we know that:

for the burning of four heretics, on April 24, 1323, the accounts of an Inquisitor from Carcassonne show the following entries:
— for large pieces of wood: 55 sols, 6 deniers;
— for branches: 21 sols, 3 deniers;
— for brush/hay:2 sols, 6 deniers;
— for four posts: 10 sols, 9 deniers;
— for rope to tie the condemned: 4 sols, 7 deniers:

– para 4 postes: 10 sols, 9 deniers;
– para cordas para amarrar os condenados: 4 sols, 7 deniers;
– para os carrascos, cada: 20 sols; 80 sols

(Baigent & Leigh, op. cit., p. 54-55)

—for the executioners, each: 20 sols; 80 sols

(Baigent & Leigh, op. cit., p. 54-55)

The Inquisitors maintained logs of dispatches in the 16th and 17th centuries in the New World. In Spanish files today, there are more than 1,000 manuscripts and 4,000 reams of loose pages that have been discovered by a current secret agency that compares past and contemporary Inquisitions.

In the Portuguese New World, the Inquisitors focused on small offenses, for example: blasphemy, sexual transgressions, superstitions, Kabala, practicing the Jewish traditions, and reading Protestant texts; as for the Catholics, the only group deemed Christian, they only sinned if they sacrificed Indians, practiced alchemy, or considered esoteric ideas.

Sarah usually visited the only library of the Delft Technische Universiteit on the days she got out of class early. Sometimes she was lucky enough to find the Professor there. One day, totally absorbed in a book in the reading room, she raised her eyes and saw him at a table near her. Surprised, she exclaimed: "How terrible!" She carried the book over to his table nearby. "Look at what is written on this page." She said, as if she had not understood the text.

"Are you in the chapter where I talk about the exile of our people?"

"Yes."

Unos cayendo, otros levantando, otros muriendo, otros nasciendo, que non habia cristiano que non ubiese dolor de ellos... (Luiz Soares in La expulsion de los judios en Espana, *p. 338)*

Some falling, others getting up, others dying, others being born, there was not a Christian that did not feel for them...
(Luiz Soares in La expulsión de los judíos en España. p. 338)

"Have a seat, Sarah."

And the Professor explained that the exodus that occurred in the 15th and 16th centuries had been a very dark part of history, as told by various historians of the men and the women, the elderly and the children, that set out on donkeys or in carts heading west, or rather, to Portugal.

These immigrants arrived in Portugal, a nation united to Spain at that time, when King Dom John IV levied a tax on the Sephardim, of eight *cruzados* per person, and a mandate for limited permanence in the country—eight months. They would, of course, at that point have to go somewhere else.

A short while later, King Ferdinand and Queen Isabella of Castile who had already realized how they could get funds for the crown with this type of transit, authorized housing for the Jews so they would return to Spain. Now they could have a house as long as they paid a ransom. This had never been done before: charging a return tax. This was a century without peace for the Jews. Some of them converted to Christianity, as a way to seek new status. However, there was a lot of confusion, for example in Morocco, where some of the Jews had to go because they had not adjusted well elsewhere. If they did not find a place to live, they would take the same route back. Many returned to the Iberian Peninsula, from where they had been exiled, but on their return this second time, though, they found themselves protected by the Inquisition tribunals themselves. Now, the "prodigal sons," since they had been converted, were received with open arms and only had to fulfill one condition—be baptized before the local bishop or his representative and other authorities of the three

...regresaran a la Península alegando que querian hacerse cristianos o presentando cerditificados de que habian recibido el bautismo. Esto obligo ao Consejo de la Inquisicion a replantear as promesas que si hicieran en el decreto de la expulsion en el 10 de novimebre de 1492" (ídem, ibidem)

"... they returned to the Peninsula alleging they wanted to become Christians or presenting baptismal certificates. This obliged the Council of the Inquisition replantear the promises made in the expulsion decree of November 10, 1492. (ídem, ibidem)

cities already designated by the same council: Badajoz, Ciudad Rodrigo, and Zamora.

Back in their homeland, the immigrants would settle in, and as a reward in the new order, their belongings were returned to them.

"Professor, here in this chapter where you mention the Council of the Inquisition redeemed itself, does that mean everyone returned?"

"No, some stayed in Morocco, and others in 1595, according to history, continued on to Hamburg, in Germany, which was one of the cities of the Hanseatic League, and thus the most mercantile in Europe at the time, with their businesses and trade of products coming from the colonies of Portugal in the New World.

"What language did they speak? How could they communicate? I imagine they spoke Spanish and German."

"No, the Ashkenazi Jews spoke Yiddish which is like an archaic German, full of Hebrew and Slovakian terms. I don't think they had any trouble in this regard. My dear Sarah, among these Sephardim there were a large number of intellectuals that dealt with learning, teaching, and indoctrination of the Jewish laws."

And then he added, "We know that among them there were some Rabbis who knew everything that was going on in the lands overseas. They were largely dedicated to science; some were doctors, dentists, physicists, and astronomers and they set up practice wherever they went. They were very articulate; some had gone to the New World already knowing that there was a land like Canaan. This land was Pernambuco in Brazil. They were also familiar with the literature of that century, and we know that they admired Lope de Vega and his theaters too.

"Who is Lope de Vega?"

"Who was he? You'll find out later."

And smiling, the Professor added, "We know that today, some of these immigrants on their pilgrimages, would repeat a little verse by Lope de Vega as if it were a rhyme or verse about life during their constant comings and goings:

> *a mis soledades voy, de mys soledades vengo, porque para andar comigo, me bastan mis pensamientos.*

They were a people that had suffered a lot, but they knew how to transcend the obstacles that appeared in their path.

Sarah laughed, even without understanding or knowing who Lope de Vega was, and the Professor laughed too, as he went back to his readings.

RABINO – Menasseh Ben Israel, baptized as Manoel Dias Soeiro (1604-1657), born in Madeira, author of works on theology and philosophy; he was *interlocutor* for Padre Vieira during his time in Holland. (by Rembrandt, 1636)

These episodes that instigated the immigration of the Sephardim, occurred many times, and all of these phenomena took place after the rebellion caused by the Union of the Seven Provinces.

From 1570 to 1621, the Jews that were in Portugal also moved to Amsterdam, in Holland, a city that at that time was experiencing tremendous growth, exploring trade from the colonies and trying to take the sugar economy from Portugal and Spain. Holland at that time had the international trade hegemony.

They were still in the library and the Professor pointed to an important passage: "If you are interested, the author Maria Antonia Bel Bravo says that the issue of the transit and settling of the Jews among the intellectuals of the 17th century, was very important from a social point of view:

Durante sus primeras décadas de existência, la comunidad amsterdanesa conto con la presencia de autoridades rabinicas... Joseph Prado...Saul Levi Mortera, de origem ashkenazi...Isaac Aboab da Fonseca, grande adepto de la cabala... Menasseh Ben Israel que gozo de grand reputacion entre teólogos y hombres de letras en el mundo Cristiano occidental...fue, ademas, el dueno de la primera imprenta judia en Amsterdã y en ella imprimio sus libros en hebreu, español, portugues e latin...Otro rabino coetano fue Moseh Rafael d'Aguilar, que junto con Isaac Aboab da Fonseca ejercio en la comunidad serfadi del noreste brasilero durante la corta ocupacion holandesa. (apud Maria Antonia Bel Bravo, in Los Sefardis em Europa, p. 70)

> *In its first decades of existence, the community of Amsterdam included Rabbinical authorities... Joseph Prado... Saul Levi Mortera, of Ashkenazi origin... Isaac Aboab da Fonseca, great adept of the Kabala... Menasseh Ben Israel, highly regarded among theologians and intellectuals in the Western Christian world... who was also the owner of the first Jewish printing press in Amsterdam where he printed his books in Hebrew, Spanish, Portuguese, and Latin... Another Coctano Rabbi was Moseh Rafael d'Aguilar, who worked with Isaac Aboab da Fonseca in the Sephardic community in northeastern Brazil during the Dutch occupation. (apud Maria Antonia Bel Bravo, in Los Sefardis em Europa, p. 70)*

"Sarah, I want to tell you this story so you can better understand this subject that so much interests you—the history of your ancestors. Your ancestors were among these immigrants who went from Portugal to Amsterdam and other places in Holland. If you count backwards, in 50-year periods, to the 1600s, you will find there have been ten generations up to yours. The couple that formed your family was young, altruistic, well educated, and from what we know, very active

D. JOÃO IV – Engraving by A. J. Quintos.

within the Antwerp and Recife communities during the time of the Inquisition. They were Portuguese. They were also the same age: 22, and they had married in the Portuguese nation of Antwerp, when they lived there with their parents.

"What was her name?"

"Sarah. You inherited her name."

"And his name?"

"Abraham."

"What did they do?"

"The diaries from that time, as well as some of the records I have seen, say that she was a sewing and embroidery teacher for children. She also taught some of them how to play the virginal, a string instrument similar to the harpsichord, which she had learned from her grandmother in Portugal. Abraham was a bookkeeper and he made maps, for King Dom John IV, when he was in Portugal, as well as for the WIC, in Delft. Abraham, according to records and documents, was a very lucky person in those days. He was the right man at the right time. He knew the Kabala and astrology very well, and he studied the reports of the navigators and explorers of the times. The Portuguese, great navigators bent on discovering the sea route to India, had a great need for his profession as keeper of records and designer of maps."

He continued explaining: "The maps were very valuable items in those days; they were ordered by the King and made by very carefully chosen persons, so that these trips could fulfill their objectives, which were to dominate the trade of specialty goods. They claimed as their domains, the lands and places they conquered, so that the rest of the world would 'know who's who…."

The times were very tumultuous, and many had their eyes on the voyages for discovery of new routes or lands. There was a lot of pirating, thievery and all types of kidnappings and robbery, including of maps. Both King John IV of Portugal, as well as King Phillip II in Spain, had as these designers of maps, their private counselors, who were loyal and completely trustworthy.

"How did they draw these maps?"

"Well, remember that they had lived in Amberes, in Portugal, long before they went to Holland? The King had heard about Abraham's skills and requested his presence in the court immediately. In the interview he asked a number of questions, for example, how he had learned this art, what his experience was, and if he had a sample map he could show him. The King was very curious to see his work especially because he was so young. Abraham showed him some of his maps, made when he was 18 to 21 years old, tutored by his grandfather. He continued honing his skills with his father, with whom he had lived before he had married. The maps showed the trips around the Iberian Peninsula, where he and his grandfather, a scientist (an astronomer), had taught him to find his way according to the celestial map."

"In this particular map, Abraham presented the route along the coast of Southern Spain, where they had reached the sea by the Guadiana River and then headed west. Following a scale they had established, according to the surface of the papyrus on which they worked, they drew the curves of the margins of the rivers and the sea coast up to the point where they had moved out to sea, when they then oriented themselves according to the heavens. They knew how to use the astrolabe and had one made by his father. This all occurred in the latter 1640s."

"The King was very interested and asked the prodigious young man especially about the geographical features he had put on the map. Around the outer margins, which framed the map, were birds, rare animals, many scientific names, and numbers. Abraham answered the questions with great confidence, thus proving the map was a true representation."

"To make a long story short, The King was convinced, and sent him on a trip to Holland, for which he asked permission to take his young wife. On this particular trip, which was the last the couple took together from Portugal, he went with Captain Joaquim Cabral, on his main ship. There were three ships in the fleet and it took three days to go from Antwerp to Delft."

DE LAET – (1581-1650), founder of the first WIC, picture published in the Historie Ofte Iaerlyck Verhael – Iconographisch Bureau, Den Haag.

"In the second half of the 16th century and the beginning of the 17th century, the confiscation of Dutch ships by Phillip II, King of Spain and Portugal, forced the Batavos to venture out to sea in search of the source of the spices from India, which resulted in the West India Company, in 1621, organized along the same lines as the East India Company, already in existence since 1602."

Chapter – A new adventure

The Dutch ships docked almost daily at the ports of Itamaracá and Igarassu, coming from Africa over the Atlantic Ocean in an attempt to keep the financial woes of the WIC afloat, with the trade of slaves from Africa and sugar from Pernambuco exported to Europe.

In 1624, there were Dutch up and down the northeastern coast of Brazil. They had attacked Bahia several times, but to no avail. A few years later they landed at Pau Amarelo, a beautiful beach, currently in the municipal district of Paulista, approximately 10 km out of Recife. Pau Amarelo, which means 'yellow wood,' is named after a tree in that part of the Atlantic Forest in Pernambuco, having a yellow trunk and yellow flowers.

The Dutch were invading and deforesting the coastal area, in an effort to conquer lands along the northeastern shores of Brazil. Chaos was the normal state of affairs, except during the time of Count Mauritius van Nassau. After 19 years, the WIC was beginning to flounder.

In 1640, trying to recuperate the great losses and the declining colonies around the Caribbean countries of Barbados and Curaçao, northeastern Brazil, and what is now territory in the United States, the WIC made one more attempt at survival, and sent a squadron that left from Rotterdam for Chile, to search for gold.

Today historians concur that Willem Usselinx, a successful merchant from Antwerp, lacked sound leadership and common sense in his endeavors to colonize South America, the West Indies, and North America. Many ships were lost to pirates on the high seas due to the ambitious seeking of routes which were a contributing factor to the failure of these undertakings. It was inevitable the Dutch would lose Brazil. Even so, struggling to keep their heads above water, they continued making voyages to Pernambuco.

It was in this same year (1640) that the fleet of ten ships set sail from Rotterdam. Heading up the main ship, the Zutphen, was the Commander and renowned Admiral Joost Banker of the WIC and other worthy individuals. Among them was one of its log keepers, the young cartographer, Abraham Dias Fernandes, who had been offered respectable remuneration for his services, and his young wife Sarah.

The voyage would take approximately four months, and he was given assurance of his position for the return voyage also.

Sarah dreamed about the New World, having received glowing news from Sephardic friends who enjoyed living in the tropics, and more especially, being part of Count Mauritius van Nassau's administration, in the flourishing town of Mauricia. The Count had understood the workings of the sugar-cane economy; realizing he needed the know-how of the Jews. He was very liberal towards them. According to Sarah and Abraham's relatives already settled in Pernambuco, he accepted and knew how to abide with any religion or sect in his government, as long as money was brought in.

RABINO ABOAB – Isaac Aboab da Fonseca (1605-1693), first Rabbi in the New World and in Brazil, born in Viseu, Portugal, the first Jewish author in the Americas.

RUA DOS JUDEUS (Jew's Street) – Thus named (Jodenstraat), in 1636. At the end of the street was the slave market (Slavenmarkt), also a place of residence for some of the wealthiest merchants, such as Gaspar Francisco da Costa, Moisés Navarro, Abraham Azevedo, and David Sênior Coronel, also called Duarte Saraiva, who hosted in his home, before 1636, the primitive synagogue that preceded K. K. Zur Israel. Watercolor by Zacharials Wagener (1634-1641).

They had also heard about the Kahal Zur Israel synagogue, erected in 1636, on the Rua dos Judeus, near the port of Aldeia dos Arrecifes (Reef Village), later to lend its name to Recife.

The old quarter, where the local merchants congregated, was near the docks in the port. This was the center of trade, where the population at that time in the 17th century, consisted of six thousand people, including French, English, Scots, Jews, Dutch, Portuguese, and *Mestiços* (half-castes).

They lived alongside each other in harmony.

Arriving with or after the Dutch were merchants, soldiers, clergy, and mascates (hawkers). The settlers already established in the province since the days of the Duarte Coelho capitancy, included Portuguese, Brazilians, and Jews—New Christians who were growers of sugar cane and producers of sugar, and also a few religious persons or Rabbis.

The Dutch did not adapt well to cultivating sugar cane. All of this had been passed on to Sarah and Abraham by their relatives who had gone before them to 'Pernambuco, in the 16th century, one of 500 Jewish families arriving in Recife, along with Rabbi Isaac da Fonseca.

The young couple was eager to see for themselves the abundant produce in the land previously described to them. Their hearts were set, however, on acquiring a sugar mill in the Zona da Mata area of Pernambuco, a very profitable business in Europe at that time. The captain of the ship, however, was not aware of their dreams.

It should be pointed out that the arrival of the sugar cane, the *criolla*, in Pernambuco's Zona da Mata, revolutionized a portion of the colony, establishing its first economic cycle.

The oldest records of sugar cane cultivation date back to 1526. Chroniclers of the time wrote that the first *engenho de açúcar* in Brazil was built shortly thereafter, in 1532, in the São Vicente capitancy, and was named Engenho do Governador. The first head of the Pernambuco capitancy, Duarte Coelho, was very astute, for as soon as he realized that the high humidity of the climate and the clayish soil were suitable for the crop, he invested in bringing Jews over from the Madeira and São Tomé Islands, aware they had the knowledge and skills to produce sugar.

Many of them had been foremen on the Islands and could run an *engenho* anywhere in the world.

The first to arrive in Pernambuco in 1550, was Diogo Fernandes, a New Christian from Portugal. He was part owner and manager of the Camaragibe *engenho.*

O engenho de São Tiago, e que pertencia aos cristãos-novos Diogo Fernandes e Branca Dias, além de outros sócios de mesma fé.

(registra Jose Alexandre Ribemboim, in Senhores de Engenho, *2000, p.55)*

The São Tiago engenho, which belonged to the New Christians Diogo Fernandes and Branca Dias besides others of the same faith.

(records José Alexandre Ribemboim, in Senhores de Engenho, *ed,..., 19..., p.55)*

Sarah and Abraham's ancestors had already become owners of this engenho in Pernambuco on the banks of the Camaragibe River.

Some believed that El Rey of Portugal had already developed a plan of action against the Dutch government in Europe. All Abraham knew, however, was that he couldn't fail the King, who counted on his maps to strategize his incursions, not only against Spain, but against Holland as well, in the near future.

Meanwhile in the royal Court of Portugal, it was rumored that the king, Dom John IV, in a ploy to restore the crown's sovereignty, was already holding secret talks with the governors in Brazil. More particularly, he was confabulating with Father Antônio Vieira, who kept him informed of Prince Mauritius van Nassau's every move, as well as the scheming among the Portuguese and Brazilians to restore the province to the Portuguese crown.

Ao mesmo tempo na corte de Portugal já se comentava que o Rei Dom João IV, em tentativa de restaurar a Coroa, mantinha, na época, conversações secretas com os governantes brasileiros e principalmente com o Pe. Antônio Vieira, que lhe deixava informado não só de todos os passos do Príncipe Maurício de Nassau, como do complô em direção à retomada do governo pelos portugueses e brasileiros.

After being dispatched to Aragon and Catalonia by Dom John IV to befriend the map makers at the service of the royal Court, Abraham made every attempt to get his hands on the true and legitimate maps of the lands conquered by Spain, in the search for gold in the New World.

He was finally able to gain access to the inner circles of the Court. He had met Jews in the local community, and all was going according to plan, until the Count of Olivares began to suspect him. He found out that he was from a family of cartographers and from then on, he placed the young couple under surveillance.

Sarah, more levelheaded than Abraham, suggested that they flee.

Greatly fearing persecution by the Count who hounded them more closely at every move they made, they finally decided to flee to the Basque country. The plan was to reach the Gulf of Biscay. At the port of Donostia (San Sebastian), they were able to take a chalupa, a small boat, arriving in Delft two weeks later. They never returned to Portugal: they did not have the courage to face Portugal's irate El Rey.

Abraham had departed unaware of two major events that had taken place in 1640. The first was that the Duke of Olivares, Gaspar de Guzman, had been deposed by the Queen of Catalonia, the playwright Quevedo taking the opportunity to lampoon him in his satire O guardanapo do rei (The king's serviette).

The second was an uprising in Lisbon in 1640, which proclaimed Portugal once again independent of Spain, though the latter only officially acknowledged its independence in 1668, when the Treaty of Lisbon was signed.

In Delft, Abraham and Sarah lodged at a small inn near the docks for a few florins, worth about one ducat.

Holland was considered the most liberal country in Europe. For example, a clergyman could receive guests without having to go through the papal bureaucracy.

The young couple found Delft charming, but were disappointed for they had not found any relatives in the town.

Touring the town, they were impressed by the number of tombs in the local cathedral, Oude Kerk. It was the oldest church in Delft, built around 1200, on Rua Heilige Geestkerkhof between two canals.

The following day was Easter Sunday and Delft's townsfolk were eagerly awaiting the celebration. After a long day, tired, they made their way back to the hostel. As fate would have it, at this same place where Abraham and Sarah were staying, actually at the same table they were having hot onion soup, trying to warm themselves so they could sleep on that cold night in April, sat another guest—a man talking about a voyage to the New World that was going to take place in the next couple of days.

It was Saturday, the day before Easter.

The elderly gentleman was going on and on at the table to whomever would lend him an ear. He was a sea wolf, an old adventurer bent on making a long voyage like this once more.

Sarah's curiosity was aroused when she heard the expression New World. "Where is this New World?"

"I've heard that they are going to Curacao in the Caribbean Sea, to Pernambuco in northeastern Brazil," he said, "and on this trip for the first time, as far as Chile, for gold.

"Pernambuco?" Sarah, asked, "And how long does it take to get there? I have relatives there."

"About three to four months, at least," he replied. "The ship will stop along the way and will be heavily loaded as usual. Have you every been on a voyage like this?"

"No, but I would really like to," Abraham answered.

"Well, if you are interested, I can ask my son to harness his horse and buggy and we can go to Rotterdam. It'll be about a five-hour trip. What is your profession?" he asked Abraham.

"I'm a log keeper, a cartographer, and an astrologist."

"Where did you learn these skills?"

"With my Grandfather in Portugal."

"Oh! Is he Portuguese? Does he speak Dutch too?"

"My ancestors went back and forth, for several years, between Holland and Portugal, where my family always worked at designing maps. Yes, we speak a little Dutch."

"Not just a little. You speak it very well. So, what do you think? Shall we embark on this venture tomorrow? Who knows? We may even find work for you."

Sarah, hardly believing what was happening, looked at her husband, nodding her head in approval.

"We are very tired at the moment and need to get some sleep. Only if it's not before nine tomorrow."

"At nine it is then. I'm going to go to my son's house now to set everything up. The clock is ticking—it's already after seven."

"Good night, then, Sir."

"Good night."

The couple that owned the inn approached the table as they stood up, exhausted by the day's activities, ready to turn in for the night.

"Good night, Ma'am."

"Good night; second door to the right; just push it open."

"Abraham, however much we would like to go on this trip to the New World, the idea is virtually impossible."

"If that's the way you feel about it we can return to Portugal. Now, if you really think about it, when will we ever have an opportunity like this again? This is our chance to go to Pernambuco and see our relatives there. We could raise our children in a good environment and even own an *engenho* in the future."

"And how would we explain this decision to our parents?"

"They will understand our leaving."

"Well, we could leave a letter with the son of the gentleman who is coming to fetch us tomorrow morning, just a few lines so they won't be worried."

"Yes. That's what we should do. Now, let's try to get some sleep."

At daybreak the bells were tolling and there was a lot of hustle and bustle outside the hotel. Entire families were flocking to the local churches: all the couples in their Sunday best, the women wearing long dark shawls from head to toe over their long skirts, with huiks on their heads protecting them from the cold.

It was a clear and beautiful day, a crisp, chilly morning without a cloud in the sky. The men in their sober apparel and broad-brimmed hats led the children along the streets of the canal-crossed town.

Some, like the Calvinists and other Protestants, were on their way to services. Others were going to the Catholic masses.

It was Easter Sunday, one of the two Sundays each year the churches can justify their presence to the faithful brethren. This is the greatest feast of Christianity.

Abraham and Sarah awoke early to the sounds of trotting hoofs and carriage wheels and the footsteps of the passersby.

The owner of the inn had already set out tea, milk, and bread for large number of guests, in the same room they had eaten the evening before.

And that's where they headed.

"Abraham, I think I'm getting kind of scared to go on this trip," Sarah said.

"There now, don't worry. I think it will be good for us. If we succeed, we will become very wealthy and can later on send back for our parents, or visit them often. And speaking about our parents, I've already written a few lines to them."

"What did you write? They're going to be very worried about us; maybe we should write when we get there."

"I don't think so," he said. "They know how close we are and that we will look after each other.

And besides, we have relatives on the other side, in the New World I mean. We'll never be alone. If things don't work out, we can always return. I'm also letting them know that it takes about four months to get to Pernambuco."

Suddenly the same elderly gentleman, the sailor they had visited with the previous evening, and his son, came into the dining room. His son, young and friendly, about Abraham's age, was the coachman.

"Good morning. Did you sleep well?" The gentleman had spotted them immediately.

"Yes. We only awoke when the bells started tolling, calling the faithful to go to church."

"I'm Abraham and this is my wife, Sarah. We didn't introduce ourselves yesterday."

The gentleman started up another conversation: "Do you know that today is a good day to go to Rotterdam, Abraham? Today, the families here have the custom of all getting together in town where the great festivities will be. Those that live in the country will be coming to Delft, so we'll have the roads to ourselves. There's nothing to worry about. Are you already packed up?"

"We don't have much with us because we had only planned on a six-day trip. Oh! Before I forget—I have a letter that I would like to send to Portugal to our parents. Do you think your son could take care of it for us?"

"Sure. Tomorrow morning I'll put it on a ship," answered the old rover's son.

"As for your having little clothing, that's not a problem. You'll be able to find something at the stops the ship will make, which will be quite a few, I'm sure. Shall we go?"

"Well, this is it," Abraham said as he paid the bill, holding the hand of his confidant, Sarah.

"Why do you think this gentleman is so interested in our going on this trip, Abraham?"

"I don't know! Maybe he's thinking that if he introduces me as a cartographer, he might get the chance to go too. We just need to see if the pay is good."

They left Delft, heading out towards Rotterdam in intense, damp cold, in a four-seater carriage. It took them half an hour just to get out of town—there were so many pedestrians, the carriage could hardly make its way through the streets along the canals. They finally reached the dirt road that circled the city on its way to Rotterdam. They could have made the trip by boat, but it was much better to go by carriage.

"Look at that windmill! Isn't it beautiful!" Sarah was exclaiming. "Why isn't it turning? And what kind of flowers are those in the field?"

"It's Sunday, so the millers aren't working today. The flowers are tulips," the old sailor explained. "We began planting them between the canals and they have grown very well in our soil. They are the most popular flower in Holland—my wife sells them at the open-air market in Hippolytusbuurt. We have planted a lot of them, all different colors, around our house."

"Who purchases them?" Sarah asked.

"All of the nobles in Europe like tulips. They're expensive flowers. They require a lot of care. The bulb only blooms once a year, and the lower class can't afford to cultivate them. The nobles adore this exotic flower which was brought here from Turkey about ten years ago and is now grown here. One of our neighbors, Mr. Jacob Vosmaer, a famous artist, devotes his time to painting them and has quite a clientele among princes and princesses. He has sold many of his paintings to the State of Holland and even a vanitas to Prince Mauritius.

"How did he get the contacts to deal with the Prince?" Abraham asked, jolting from one side to side in the carriage, as the coachman flicked the whip to make the horses go faster.

"Vosmaer is a well-known captain-major in one of our civil-guard companies, and is probably a Calvinist, which carries a lot of weight.

"I see," Abraham said pensively. "Sarah, can you pass the crackers, please?"

"Wouldn't you like a pear?"

"Yes—a pear too. I'm starving," he said.

As they rode along, they gazed at the scenery in the countryside: the dairy farms where the country folk tended their cows and goats in the pastures around their houses surrounded by water. They were impressed how some of them alighted from boats loaded down with fruit and vegetables probably from the local market.

Their houses were tiny, tall, and made of bricks; the locals dressed in dark clothes. The few women in sight wore long full skirts, with the traditional aprons tied over them.

"Look how full that boat is," the old sailor was saying as he pointed to the right of the carriage.

"It must be returning from Rotterdam and is actually very lucky that the river hasn't frozen over."

"How much longer before we arrive?" Sarah asked.

"Are you already impatient, my dear? I've turned the glass over once, so we've been traveling for about four hours. We should be entering the city not too long from now."

"Are we going straight to the ship?"

"No. First we'll find an inn to spend the night and then tomorrow, on Monday, I'll try to talk with the gentleman organizing the voyage, to negotiate our passage. And before I forget: I'd like you to go with me, young man."

"Yes, of course. It's of my concern too. I wonder how many people will be on the ship...."

"Probably around a hundred."

"That's all?"

"Yes, but don't forget the ship is carrying a heavy load, usually supplies for a year, which really weighs it down."

"Whoa!" the coachman said as he reigned in the horses near the docks. "Where are we going to stay? I'll be needing you to get out so I can feed and water the horses."

"We can get out here, Pieter. There's a small inn I know on the corner."

It was already after two in the afternoon and they were all hungry and excited about this voyage. Sarah was intrigued by the beautiful buildings and houses around the canals in the city when Abraham pointed out the docks.

"How exciting! Look at all those ships—a lot more than in Antwerp."

"See that one right in front there? I think it's ours; it's the same ship that took Count Mauritius van Nassau to Pernambuco in 1636, arriving there in 1637. It's the Zutphen."

"Let's go see it up close," Sarah suggested.

"Yes, let's do. You have no idea how much I would like to travel on this ship that transported Count Nassau-Siegen to the New World, four years ago. They say it is one of the best we have, and that after the

Count's trip, when it sailed from the Texel Port for the Southern Hemisphere, it made only one other trip. After the Count arrived there in 1637, the ship went on to Africa, returning to Pernambuco to unload its cargo of slaves, then headed off to Europe to the Port of Antwerp, where it arrived in 1638. It sailed one more time following the same route, in 1639, except that on this final journey it returned to Rotterdam; this is the first time it will leave from this port.

"When are you two going to talk with the Captain? Do you know him?"

"I think so. I believe I traveled with him before, on another ship."

"How many times have you gone to the New World?" Sarah asked him.

"Twice."

"Don't you want to go and stay there?"

"I'm a little too old for that now. I settled in and raised my family here and they need me here now. It's a wonderful situation for you though. You're starting out your lives now and have relatives over there. If I were younger, I would stay and settle there. Fifty years from now the Dutch government will be very powerful in Brazil."

"Mr. Jodocus! Mr. Jodocus!" The shouts were coming from the deck of a ship. A gentleman in a cape with a large black hat was trying to get the attention of the old mariner, who was about to board the ship.

"Is your name Jodocus?" Sarah asked.

"Yes, that's right. I can hear someone calling me, but I can't tell where it's coming from."

"It's coming from the deck of that ship over there," Sarah said as she pointed.

"Heavens, if it isn't Boudewyn Hendriksz! We traveled together coming here. Two years ago he brought several Tapuia Indians from northeastern Brazil to Holland for the first time. He was all over the news in Amsterdam when he arrived."

Waving to his friend as they walked up the gangplank of the ship, he asked Sarah and Abraham, "Do you know the history of the Tapuias?"

"No."

"The Tapuias were some of the cannibal tribes that also lost their lands in Brazil. Hoping to rid themselves of the Portuguese and later on return to their lands, which the black slaves had invaded, they headed south along the shoreline (no one knows where they came from—3,000 in all—only that they came from the state of Rio Grande do Norte), planning to align themselves with the Dutch against the Portuguese. Nassau, aware of the problem that was brewing, immediately wrote their morubixaba, Jandui, to strengthen their alliance against the common enemy and reaffirmed to the Indian chief their loyal and benevolent support, stating solemnly that their fate of life or death was the same as theirs, having long ago vowed to be enemies of the Portuguese.' (Barleus, p. 189). Two thousand men joined Nassau's troops, and later, under the orders of Nassau, Captain Hendriksz took with him to Holland some of the Indians that had survived the battlefields. They were accepted in Holland for their being exotic and made their way in the handcraft markets."

"Wow! Are there still cannibals over there? Sarah asked.

"I'm not sure. There could be."

As Captain Hendriksz walked down the gangplank towards his old friend whose company he thoroughly enjoyed, he bore a wide smile on his face, expressing the happiness he was known for.

"What are you doing around here, my great man? Are you planning on joining us for this trip?"

"Yes, I am, and this time I'm also bringing along two others who are going to meet up with their family in Pernambuco."

"What is his profession?"

"He's a cartographer and an astrologist. The young couple speaks Dutch and Portuguese."

"Well, if that's the case, I believe we can already guarantee him a job. We always need this kind of courageous person to work different shifts, switching off with others during the journey. Come along and we'll speak with Joost Banker, Admiral of the ship (in *Zeeuwen en de Westindische Compagnie*, p. 62), whose actual name was Joos van Trappen (in *Diário de um Soldado*, Richshoffer). I'm one of the four officers in this fleet. I know we can use your expertise."

The three boarded the ship that was being loaded to sail on Tuesday. There were people everywhere, this being one of the more modern ships at that time, with a capacity for approximately 100 passengers, 20 sailors, 5 officers, and the *mestre de cabotagem* (navigator). They walked all the way up to the captain's quarters where they met Admiral Joost Banker, a tall 45-year-old man, with a flourishing moustache, beard, and red hair. He was seated at his table making a few notes, and hearing them knock, politely told them to enter, asking, "What can I do for you?"

Mr. Jodocus was presented as a sailor experienced in journeys to the New World, who in turn was making no secret of his great desire to go on this voyage. He presented the couple to the admiral. "These are my friends, Sarah and Abraham."

The admiral commented, "Abraham what?"

"Abraham Dias Fernandes."

"So young and already married?"

"Yes. We got married at the beginning of the year."

"Have you ever been on a long boat trip? I must advise you that if your wife is expecting, she will probably be quite uncomfortable. It's not easy to be aboard for days on end. The conditions are precarious, and hygiene and comfort are minimal."

Turning to Sarah, he asked how she would entertain herself during the trip.

"Oh, I could work with the children onboard and teach them to embroider."

"And you, Abraham, what do you know about the heavenly bodies?"

"Sir, my family in Portugal follows the tradition of making map—my Grandfather passed this profession on to me. My Great Grandfather was a well-known physicist. Regarding the celestial bodies I know some that can be seen here in the Northern Hemisphere, and their appropriate positions, which vary according to the time of year. I also know the Kabbalah, Sir."

"Well, you are very lucky—just this morning I mentioned that we would need to hire someone to switch off with our onboard log keeper and cartographer. I must confess that I was concerned that we would find someone in this short amount of time. Our Hondius is getting old."

Puffing on his pipe, he told them to bring their belongings onboard.

"Abraham, after you are settled in, come and see me so I can present you to my log keeper and map-maker friend, with whom you'll be working."

The three radiated happiness. Jodocus was only concerned now about finding his son and sending him back to Delft. Sarah and Abraham were famished because they had forgotten to eat. The news that they would already be spending the night onboard was very exciting to them, and there was little time to talk as they walked along.

They no longer needed to worry about their next move.

"Look, Jodocus, there's your son in the carriage. He must have already fed the horses."

Abraham completed the sentence with one of his playful comments: "and it took him just long enough to warm himself with a drink." The young coachman stopped near the dock, stepped down, and came over to greet his father."

"Did it work out?"

"Yes. The three of us will be leaving on Tuesday, I ran into an old friend on board. He greeted me and invited me to go along on this voyage to the New World. We have been very lucky, actually, because the ship is not yet full. Tell your Mother that I shall return by Christmas, and that I will bring her some beautiful fur to make a fine coat and also colorful feathers she likes to collect."

"Hey, Pieter, can't you take someone with you to Delft to unload the cargo?"

"I've already taken care of it, Father."

They hugged each other, the young man wishing his father a wonderful journey and expressing his great desire to also make this voyage soon.

"Good-bye."

The vessel was similar to the first Portuguese ships, but nevertheless much larger; it was a legitimate "*Driemaster in Gekartelde Cirkel, Driestip*: 130x130x12mm" (3 masts, 32 meters high). The highest level belonged to the *mestre de cabotagem*, and was referred to as the "captain's quarters." From there he controlled the ship's course, spending practically all his time between the deck and his quarters. Seeing him above, Sarah and Abraham decided to go up to meet him.

Sarah's curiosity was aroused, and she was walking ahead of Abraham who was surprised at her interest; however, when they met him, they realized he was a regular Dutchman like others on board, with his wide brimmed hat and feathers. Under his jacket he was wearing the typical wide white collar that totally covered his neck, and bombacha pants, also dark in color, that made noise as he walked from one side to the other on the deck. The couple soon left the area, and Abraham, carrying a role of maps, went to speak with Admiral Banker.

Knocking on the Admiral's door, he announced himself: "Admiral, it's Abraham."

"Enter," he responded.

The captain, with his huge mustache, seemed very pleasant, holding a book by the Dutch poet G. Brederoo, deemed a rebel at that time, especially after writing comments favoring the Jews in his theater piece *Moortje*. The Admiral, humorously asked Abraham to read a section from the book which he kept open to a particular page. "Out loud, please, so that my officers and I can hear you," he said, with a type of humor that was odd to him.

So Abraham read: "Inhumane custom! Godless rascality! That people are being sold to horselike slavery. In this city there are also, who engage in that trade. In Farnabock, but God will know." (in *The Dutch in the Atlantic Slave Trade* 1600-1815, p. 10).

When he finished reading, the Admiral asked him: "Do you like poetry? Did you like this particular part? What do think, young man? Say something."

"I don't know what to say, Sir. Perhaps I didn't really understand it because I don't know that much about these types of problems," Abraham answered, leaving the Admiral no choice but to continue the conversation.

Tradução — Costume desumano! patifaria infame! Essa gente está sendo vendida como animal para a escravidão. Nesta cidade há também quem se empenhe nesse comércio. Em Farnalock porém Deus-o sabe.

"Very well, but before you go I would like you to meet my officer Mr. Willem Hondius who has worked with us during some of our voyages and prepared interesting reports on several of them. He is also a metal engraver in his off time. Then you are free to retire to the passengers quarters. You'll be needing these candles when it gets dark. And just a reminder: if you are planning on staying in Pernambuco, you'd better find out about quilombos."

The Admiral was holding his sides with laughter.

"It's a pleasure to meet you," the young log keeper and cartographer said. I hope to learn a lot with you during this long journey. What I know I learned from my Father who studied at the *Armazem da Guine* in the last century. He was there at the same time as Mr. Lopo, Andre Homem, and Gaspar Viegas."

"It's a pleasure to meet you too, and I'm looking forward to instructing you. I'm at least twice your age, and I've had a lot of experience with this. How do you

No Hemisfério Norte, os navegadores se orientaram principalmente pela Estrela Polar. No Hemisfério Sul, passaram a usar o Cruzeiro do Sul. Para estimar as latitudes pela altura do Sol, consultavam as chamadas tábuas de declinação. (In Brasil segredo de Estado, *de Sérgio Correa da Costa)*

In the Northern Hemisphere, the navigators charted their course by the North Star. In the Southern Hemisphere they relied on the Southern Cross. To calculate latitude by the position of the Sun they used the so-called declination tables. (In Brasil segredo de Estado, de Sérgio Correa da Costa)

work with your maps? Do you have any with you so I can take a look at them?"

"Yes. This was the last one I charted, on a short trip between Porto and Lisbon, Portugal."

As he examined the young man's work, Mr. Hondius made honest comments about the details he had included in the color of the waters, notes on the winds, the stars in the sky on those particular days and nights in April, and the rivers that ran into the seas they were sailing.

"I'm sure that we're going to get along just fine, Abraham."

The young man thanked him and excused himself. He went back on deck with his wife to watch for the first time Rotterdam's sunset. From there they could also see the ships anchored at the dock, sometimes more than fifty in number.

It started to get dark and the warehouses around the dock were becoming invisible. On board, the sailors were beginning to light the torches, when all of a sudden there was a shrill whistle that gathered all of the shipmates on the deck. They came running from all directions—orders were about to be given. Sarah and Abraham decided this was a good time to go down to the passenger's quarters where most of the passengers as well as their quarters were.

As they entered the area, Sarah noticed that the women were trying to hang pieces of cloth from the ceiling to the floor, improvising curtains for divisions. Sarah and Abraham didn't have much luggage, only what was absolutely necessary—a few clothes, some linens they had received for their wedding, and Sarah's embroidery loom and threads.

Abraham's reference books, navigation instruments for making maps, and the Sefer Torah (Book of Laws, known as the Christian Pentateuch) were all packed in two large leather bags.

The entire small area of ten square meters by 1.70m in height was completely taken up. Among candles and oil lamps were several families, their children trying to cuddle up among their belongings, and a few straw mattresses spread out on the floor. There wasn't any comfort or privacy.

Sarah put on warmer clothes and said to Abraham, "You know, Abraham, this situation isn't going to bother me. I just want to be free from the uncertainty of where we are going to live and to have peace. The only thing I want now is to have our land in Pernambuco. I'm sure that we'll find stability there, and besides, our relatives have lived there for over a hundred years."

"I agree, and also I need to take good care of you until we get there, because I have a feeling there may be a baby on the way! You've been tiring easily lately, you're always saying you are sleepy, you've changed a little," he said.

"I'm just sleepier than usual, but who knows, maybe we'll be lucky enough to find a doctor or midwife on board, and I promise I'll ask them to examine me. At this point I don't think they would be able to really tell yet...."

"Maybe that won't be necessary. I would really like to have a child soon. After all, we have already been married for three months, so it's very possible you are expecting." And very gently he added, "Sarah, you haven't had your time of the month."

"My dear, I wanted to surprise you. I want to give you many children so they can work towards what will be theirs in the future—our *engenho de açúcar*. I'm sure we'll be able to establish ourselves there without being persecuted."

"We're going to work for this, Sarah, and we will make it. For now we have to try to get some sleep. We've had a long day—just today we were in an inn, in a carriage, and now on a ship."

The day dawned overcast and very cold. Visibility was low at the dock in the port, but the commander still kept his crew busy. Some were already up, having been awoken by some of the children's crying—there were quite a few children on board, a pleasure for all concerned.

From the deck, Admiral Banker was issuing the first orders of the day: "All families need to leave the ship; your belongings may remain on board; you should return no later than three in the afternoon. The ship will be loaded throughout the day to be ready for departure Tuesday morning." It was only six-thirty, Monday morning.

"Abraham, how are the families going to get around with all of their children? It's dangerous to use that rope ladder carrying a child in your arms."

"Come on, over this way," one of the fathers was yelling as he descended the ladder backwards holding a child by each of his hands, while his wife was cradling a baby in her arm.

"I'm scared to go down," she said.

"Come one, Ma'am, you need to go. There's a long line and we all have children too," another passenger complained, stepping up, well-dressed with a starched organdy collar and black hat with a plume in it, and smoking a long-stemmed pipe.

On the deck, the *mestre de cabotagem* was using his periscope as if to justify his importance. There were a lot of passengers, some of which were irritated when they discovered they would need to evacuate the ship, for they had spent the night trying to get accustomed to the rocking of the vessel.

The children had faired better than many of the adults on board who had spent the night throwing up. Others hadn't been sick, but had not slept well due to the excitement, curiosity, poor accommodations, and especially lack of privacy.

"Abraham, let's find a place to have breakfast and then go for a walk around the city."

"Good morning," an older passenger was saying to a seaman who was trying to throw water on the deck to scrub it.

"Good morning," he responded when he saw that the older gentleman had stopped and seemed to be waiting. "What can I do for you?"

"Young man, what is the best thing for nausea? I spent the night throwing up and bothering the other passengers."

"I see you haven't found your sea legs. We carry a type of very strong pepper on board that resolves the problem, but it is practically intolerable when ingested." And chuckling, he asked, "Would you like to try some piripiri in a biscuit?"

The older man hesitatingly responded, "Not just now because we are leaving the ship, but perhaps when I return." Turning to his wife he commented, "These sailors are so uncivilized—what a primitive way to deal with illncss!" repeating under his breath what the sailor had said.

"What did you say?" his wife asked.

However, when he tried to speak, his nausea returned.

"Are you going to faint again? Let's get you off the ship right now. A little fresh air will do you good. I have faith that when we return this afternoon, you will feel fine and we will be able to face the three months at sea without any problems."

"I need to tell you what the sailor said...."

"Yes, all you need to do is 'eat this medicine,' dear. I'm going to learn how to use this pepper.

I want you back in good spirits, happy and optimistic."

The vessel was slowly emptying, the passengers leaving in single file, obeying the captain's orders. They weren't going anywhere in particular because they had been surprised by this order to evacuate the ship. The men were somewhat confused; however the women, as commonly occurs when faced with the unexpected, were controlling the situation. Their 'first order of the day' was to feed their children and try to facilitate their husband's life.

As they came off the vessel, they saw a few inns and the open market around the cathedral, and that is where the ninety-five passengers headed.

The vessel could carry a hundred passengers, which were usually distributed around the *entrecobertas*, among the cannons and several hatches, in the midsection.

Below was the main hold and above, the deck. To the Dutch of the WIC, their ship was like a being that required constant care, specific tending every four hours. Time was calculated with a sandglass, marked as it was turned, at which time a bell was struck so the crew would know when it was time for the next watch.

It was a clear crisp day without any wind, and it passed quickly and pleasantly. The seamen went up and down carrying the cargo on their shoulders or rolling barrels when possible, loading supplies to last a year.

The fleet always sailed from Holland to India, and returned via the New World. Water, the main supply for the journey, was stored in large barrels; unfortunately, after a few days the taste was awful because it absorbed the flavor of the wood. The cargo consisted of Portuguese wines and aguardentes, lightly salted meat (beef, pork, and sausage), biscuits, a lot of crackers, a few other types of food, and even some live animals (pigs, sheep, and chickens) for food during the voyage. Rice, fish, and cheese were eaten only on saints' days, when meat could not be eaten; sacks of flour, grains, and dried vegetables competed for space among the other foods. Also in the hold were all the arms for protection against the emerging piracy, a great concern to all. And finally, the tools the colonists would need when they arrived in the New World were also stored there.

At four that afternoon, the crowd of colonists had already returned, ready to go onboard and settle in. The outside torches were lit and the ten vessels remained close together throughout the night.

With the first puffs of wind, the seamen raised the sails and the lead, and the Zutphen headed out towards the English Channel. The sea was calm and the ships sailed along serenely, with very favorable winds. A few of the sailors calmly fished, which attracted the curiosity of the children, who then sat patiently, waiting for the next *badejo* or *pescado* to be caught and removed from the sea. These were the tastier fish and would always be prepared for the noon meal.

The timepiece was turned once more and the bell tolled, bringing the next wave of seamen quickly to the deck.

They appeared from all directions of the vessel for their watch.

"Look at all those fish," the lookout in the crow's nest was saying to his mate coming on duty.

"Any problems?"

"I don't think so. It's just that last night the winds whipped at the cables, and all morning I've been hearing something scraping."

He took over the lookout position. The morning had arrived full force and energetic, without problems.

"What a beautiful day Abraham. It's cold but the sky is so clear. I would like to find a little space on deck with a chair and embroider a little," Sarah said enthusiastically.

"Let's see what we can do about that," Abraham responded as they were walking up to the deck. I don't know if you'll be able to sit out here very long though—it's quite windy."

"Hello there, Abraham," Hondius remarked as he spotted them. "I'm going on duty now, and I'll hand things over to you the next shift." He went below to the large stateroom for his watch as log keeper of the ship. His job was to record all the happenings during the voyage, and the Admiral was very wordy in his speech.

"Abraham, don't forget your notations—you may need to make another map," Sarah remarked, reminding him this was what he was being paid for.

"My dear, I always have the copy of my *Orbis Typus Universalis Tabula* of 1512 with me, and also my astrolabe. You have no idea how curious I am to see the Southern Cross and other constellations in the Southern Hemisphere, or even discover new ones, Sarah."

At that moment Hondius returned to the deck, with his hands full of fishing hooks for the couple, so they could enjoy a few hours of fishing. Abraham, smiling, thanked him and turned to Sarah, asking, "Did you know that Mr. Hondius is also a metal engraver? He produces the most beautiful copper maps I have ever seen; and look at what else he makes with his pliers—fishing hooks, hinges, and other things needed on board."

"That's wonderful. Do you make them in different sizes and shapes?"

"Yes, that's how I keep busy sometimes when I'm at sea! But what I really like to work on is copper maps with their frontispieces and heraldic ornamental motifs, which I learned from some Portuguese from the Escola de Sagres. Ma'am, here, keep some of these hooks and enjoy yourself fishing," Hondius said, handing them a number of fishing hooks.

"I'm feeling a little sick. I think I'll go below deck to our quarters in the *entrecoberta*."

The children ran around noisily in that small space between the hold and the deck, and the older sisters kept an eye on their younger brothers and sisters and followed them wherever they went.

It was difficult for the passengers, who on one hand had to adhere to the exacting orders of Admiral Joost Banker, a strict military disciplinarian of the Nassaus, and on the other hand take care of their families.

Banker liked going to the New World, also referred to as the West Indies (only later called America). For each successful voyage, which included going to northeastern Brazil and delivering a solid report to the Nassaus in Holland, he received a commendation and an increase in salary, thus guaranteeing his retirement, for which he already had plans—a number of acres for a tulip farm near Keukenhof.

Night fell, and once again Captain Banker's voice rang out: "All guards to your posts, port and starboard lanterns lit, those not on watch to your quarters, maintain silence on the deck, wake-up bell at six."

In the meantime the passengers were getting in line in the ship's galley for their 'chow.'

"No! Don't bring the children!" one of the passengers was saying to his wife, who wanted them all to get in line.

There actually were a good number of children on board—around twenty-eight--and about twenty were less than five years old.

"I'll take the food to you in our room, Dear."

"What do you mean room," the woman retorted. "It's a dump!"

"You shouldn't be complaining! Now, just take the children with you and calm them down. I'll be there with the food in a few minutes."

"And what are we having for supper?" she asked furiously. "We can't even bathe the children, and they're so filthy."

"Please go to our quarters! You knew this voyage was going to be difficult, but you insisted on coming!"

The woman turned around and followed the others who were also returning with their children to their quarters.

There were five sailors in charge of making and serving the food in the galley. On the first day, the evening meal was somewhat disorganized; however, the following morning things went more smoothly—breakfast was a generous serving of dried biscuits, crackers, sausage, oatmeal, and tea.

On the second day, the three large pots contained vegetable soup, meat and boiled potatoes, and rice. The food had no fat or oil in it, because they believed that fatty foods brought on seasickness (nausea). Each person in line extended their plate to the sailors serving the food, who in turn gave them a ladleful from each pot, as well as a mug of hot soup. Mr. Roiz, one of the passengers, went through the line three times, because he had his wife and three children to feed, and he was spilling half of the contents of soup from the mugs as he carried them.

Generally, many of the passengers did not eat—they were so seasick they were practically "throwing up their souls." Quite a few of them had already heard about the *emparedado de piripiri*, but no one was courageous enough to try it.

The following morning, as the ship entered the English Channel, the winds were blowing favorably NWW. The bell tolled at five—it was still dark—and the crew scurried to their posts.

There were six watches, which changed every four hours, according to the monthly schedule set by the Captain.

As usual, breakfast was served at six and was quite generous. The torches were still lit and could be seen from the other ships.

All of the men on the ship were in line, while the women took care of cleaning their quarters, the only space provided for the passengers. Sanitary conditions were quite precarious due to the crowding together of so many people in such a small area; cleanliness was practically impossible. To make matters worse, they couldn't even bathe, having to wet a towel in the ocean water and just wipe the children when it was time for them to go to bed or before putting on clean clothes. The women soon learned they had to wash their clothes in ocean water, which gutted the soap because of the high salt content in the water. The clothes were hung on short improvised lines in front of the portholes, which had to be opened during the day to air out the quarters, and were left open on sunny days for longer periods.

"What do you have to say about your experience with us so far, Abraham? You were on watch last night, weren't you?" asked Mr. Hondius.

"Very interesting. I recorded a few stars further south, but I haven't had a chance to look them up in the *Orbis Typus Universalis Tabula*, from 1512, where terra brasilis is.

"Just wait 'til we get to the Southern Hemisphere—you're going to be in awe at how beautiful the celestial map is—many of the constellations are visible to the naked eye this time of year."

"I've read a lot about this in the Kabbalah, Mr. Hondius."

"So have I. As a matter of fact, I have that book. But now you are going to experience the real thing. Use this opportunity well and make your own maps. Draw the routes carefully, and then keep your map. You can reproduce it in Europe or even in the New World, and put it up for sale."

"You know, Mr. Hondius, I really am looking for a new life. That's why I'm going to a new land, more specifically to Pernambuco. I'm going to be working at an *engenho de açúcar* that belongs to some of my relatives."

"Which *engenho* is it? I visited some that were sold to those of the land, between 1637 and 1638. Have you heard that some of the *engenhos* were burned down by a man who is well known in the area?"

"Who?"

"Matias de Albuquerque. I actually met him when I took Count Mauritius van Nassau to the port of Recife in 1637."

"The *engenho* that belongs to my relatives is the Camaragibe. They have slaves. And many have already been accepted in society there. We have been told that the blacks, for example, are essential to the *engenho*, which is water-powered."

"As I was saying, I was there when 149 *engenhos* were burned and abandoned. 65 of those that were abandoned were later confiscated and sold by the Dutch authorities to Portuguese, Jewish, Brazilian, and Dutch residents in the area. Where exactly is this *engenho*?"

"Going up the Capibaribe River, after the várzea (flat area along the river) where Matias de Albuquerque fought with our relatives, and set up his second camp."

"Yes. I know that all of the *engenhos* are just a few leagues from the coast, the strip of land most appropriate for cultivating sugar cane That soil is so rich that the WIC decided to invest in the sugar trade, believing it would last for a number of years. The Capibaribe River runs through it, and there are many slaves *metedores de lenhas* (who feed the large ovens with wood) and in the ox carts, for the amount of sugar produced at this *engenho* last year was 10,000 *arrobas* (one arroba = 15 kilos) of sugar."

"How do you know so much about *engenhos*?"

"I learned how to plant sugar cane and produce sugar when I was living in the Azores."

"Is this *engenho* one of the 65?"

"No, it was already theirs. They've owned it since the 16th century. After the burnings they were lucky to be able to remain there, and three years ago they started replanting the sugar cane."

"What will you be doing there?"

"I'm not really sure, but I may work at the *passo* at the dock, in charge of storing the sugar that will probably be sent to Holland."

"Do you think that's possible if Governor Nassau's escabinos are in charge of the district, for example, importing and exporting the sugar and pau-brasil?"

"I don't know exactly how it's going to work out, but I think I'm going to be helping my Uncle receive the goods to maintain the slaves, or maybe purchase the slaves, or perhaps receive supplies from Europe, such as olive oil, cod, copper, iron, and tin."

Hondius was satisfied with his answer, when suddenly Sarah appeared on deck, looking as if she was somewhat uncomfortable, and asked politely, "What time to you go on watch today?"

"I don't have to work today, Sarah. Why?"

"I'm not feeling very well, and I would really like you to stay with me."

"Go ahead, Abraham You have a whole life ahead of you to dream of and to build," Hondius said.

Excusing himself, Abraham accompanied Sarah to their quarters, if they could be referred to as such.

"I'm feeling very nauseous today. I can't even lie down because the rocking of the ship is giving me a headache."

"Would you like to try some *emparedado de piripiri*?"

"Yes."

"I'll see if I can get some in the galley," Jacob told her.

In the meantime, the little girls had surrounded Sarah, begging her to teach them to embroider. She had already noticed the number of young girls between six and fifteen who were very bored, and had purposely placed her embroidery looms and little basket with thread that she carried in her sewing apron so they could be seen. This was her strategy to attract the mothers and their daughters.

"Here you are, Dear; I was able to get the emparedado. Just promise me that you'll eat it slowly." Admiring Sarah's courage, he watched as she took her first bite, but then became concerned as tears welled up in her eyes and streamed down her cheeks.

"Are you going to be able to digest this, Sarah?"

Her mouth was on fire from the pepper, but she was able to take it: "I don't know. Can you get me a glass of water?"

She coughed and fretted until Abraham returned with the water, then together they took it easy.

Captain Banker's voice could be heard up on the deck, announcing their arrival at the English Channel.

This was the first part of the fleet's route. The following day they would be passing Dunkirk if all went well.

A few minutes later, Sarah, now lying down, turned to her husband and said, "Abraham, I don't feel nauseous anymore, but I'm not feeling well. My stomach is burning terribly. I need some fresh air."

"Let's go for a walk up on the deck then, before turning in for the evening. It'll be dark soon, and it's getting cold."

It was stormy throughout the night and morning dawned cold with a choppy sea. The storm, however, had moved on. The ship was being tossed around by the waves, NW to SWW, rocking from one side to the other, but this time Sarah did not complain about the nausea.

She had awakened ready to have a different and better day. She carried a chair over to one of the portholes and started to embroider. She was soon surrounded by mothers and daughters, who curiously asked if she would be willing to teach them.

"Sure," she replied. "All you will need is some thread, talagarça (loosely woven cloth), needles, and patience."

"What's your name?" Sarah asked a little girl who was curiously watching her use the embroidery loom.

"Maria," she replied. "What's that?" she asked, pointing.

"It's an embroidery loom." Sarah took it apart to show her how to put the embroidery cloth, with the design already traced on it, in the frame.

"Have you ever embroidered anything, even without an embroidery loom?"

"No, but I have a thimble my Grandmother gave me."

"That's nice. The thimble protects you from sticking yourself with the needle when you are embroidering with the loom."

"But I don't have a loom and I don't have any cloth either."

"I'll lend you mine."

"And what about the design? How can I get that?"

"I'll draw it for you. What would you like to embroider first?"

"A house. My house to be in Pernambuco."

"Alright. How about if I draw a house near a river, and then we embroider together?"

"I want to embroider too!"

"Me too!"

One by one the young girls gathered around Sarah, who was very friendly and kind to them. They all wanted one of the cloths she had drawn on, and after those were gone, she passed out the others so they could create their own designs to embroider. There weren't enough for all of them, so a few of the young girls went to ask their mothers for a handkerchief or even just a piece of a sheet so they could participate too.

Sarah had improved the spirits of at least half of those on the ship with her talents and had also helped some of the mothers with their younger children as well.

Even though the environment was terrible and was not clean, they tried to focus their attention elsewhere. They began visiting with each other and within a few days knew each other by name.

There were ten families with children on board the Zutphen besides Sarah and Abraham—all of them headed to the Dutch colony in Pernambuco. These families had been selected by the WIC in Amsterdam, Rotterdam, Brest, Tesel, and Delft. They had worked the land in Holland and were now willing to follow the orders of the new governor in Brazil, Count Mauritius van Nassau: "Whatever the Dutch conquered or hoped to conquer, he would... provide military patents for those that were most deserving; in times of peace or war... he would make decisions concerning honors and civil function..." (Barleus).

When the bell tolled at the end of the afternoon, the men and women who had now adapted to being on board responded to the call for chowtime and stood side by side in line before the large pots in the kitchen with their tin plates and cups, waiting to be served.

Another day passed in relatively calm seas, when suddenly other ships began to surround the Zutphen, the main ship. The torches and lanterns were all lit, and the ships were tossed about violently by the angry sea. The sailors struggled with buckets, bailing the water that had come on board, and the passengers were so frightened by the storm that they withdrew to their quarters earlier than usual. Some prayed, others held their children, and still others were so seasick they were throwing up, even if they hadn't eaten. This was the first storm they had encountered, caused by the late spring and their passing near the rocky cliffs.

It was almost May, the time of year for strong winds which blew SWE, NEW, or SES. It stormed for two nights and three days, and when it was over, two of the ships had been lost, a few sailors were never seen again, and many goods earmarked for the city of Maurícia had been washed overboard.

Captain Banker, however, notified his crew that he was at his post and alert, praying while awaiting Divine Providence to grant him permission to set off to Cape Verde, which would be a long stretch of sailing. Yet, the Captain could not completely hide his anguish at their losses and conditions after the storm.

The Zutphen was sitting low in the water and could even sink. Abraham, using the situation to his advantage, hung around Mr. Hondius seeking his guidance concerning his map, especially the directions of the winds. He needed to document these winds, which were the main problem at the moment.

The old sailor told him that this passage through the English Channel was always dangerous, and that they—he and Captain Banker—had experienced this before. They had gone this same route together three years ago, in the same ship, with Prince Nassau.

"Look, Captain! We're being tossed against the Sorlingas, these terrible rocks."

"I know that this is an extraordinary and terrifying experience for you, Abraham, but I assure you that we will come through it all right. You should be using some instrument to measure the wind so we can record it on the map.

"I would like to spend more time at this, but Sarah is seasick again and needs my attention too. We could lose the baby. As you know, even the water that we have to drink..., it's a nightmare."

"Yes, it is serious, and we still have a good eighty days at sea ahead of us until we get to our destination."

"But we'll be making a stop at the Cape Verde Islands, right?"

"The way things are going, we'll be stopping some place around here. If the Captain doesn't, some of the ships might not make it."

Things had finally become somewhat stable, when the main ship began to roll about again. All of the passengers tried to huddle together to get warm—the waves hitting the vessel were continuously spraying them with cold water.

It was pitch black, so the horizon could no longer be seen, and there were twenty-meter waves

BANKER – Engraving reproduced in the book "Zeeuwen en de Westindische Compagnie", by Doeke Roos.

threatening to throw the ships against the rocks. Two of them, the most laden with supplies for the colony, not able to maneuver in time, actually hit the rocks. The passengers could hear the sailors shouting for help in the middle of the darkness and deafening sound of the waves. They had already experienced at least one storm at sea, but were still quite frightened since they had only been aboard for a few days. The ships kept changing directions to find the best winds, sometimes NWN, other times SW: it was horrible.

Avoiding going too near the rocks, the crews on the other ships tried to find the wreckages and possible survivors. Many had survived and were pulled from the sea.

This was a difficult task, taking the eight remaining vessels approximately five hours to complete the maneuver.

The main ship, Zutphen, was idling, and the other eight had dispersed. The Captain decided to stay nearer the coast to find Falmouth village in the English Channel.

Captain Banker suddenly announced that they would be going to Falmouth, where they would take down the sails, drop the anchors, and everyone was to leave the ship.

There they remained for a good three days, while it rained continuously.

They couldn't keep up with bailing water from the holds—the more they removed, the more came in from the upper deck. One of the sailors lost his life due to hypothermia; before he was thrown overboard he was awarded the honors he would have received in his country. Netcher, in *Les Hollandais au Brésil*, wrote that "the soldiers of the company were mainly German,

Italian, French, and Irish mercenaries, outcasts of society that had no other objective than to pillage. The sailors mostly Dutch and more carefully recruited, were more moderate and disciplined."

The townspeople where they had anchored were very generous. Two of the churches removed furniture from rooms to accommodate the passengers from the Zutphen, spreading horse hair mattresses on the floor for them. They gathered together in family units, using the available space as best they could. Towels, blankets, sheets, and warm food were brought by the faithful of the town of Falmouth—they knew how to coordinate in times of need.

The Captain and his crew were either on their ships, or in the small quarters in the warehouses at the dock. Three days went by before the seas became calm. The winds finally died down and around three in the afternoon, the skies began to clear up, with the sun timidly peering through the clouds. There was only a slight breeze from the West. The experienced Captain gave orders for all passengers to board, which they did, and spend the night on the ship, for the plan was to set sail early the following day.

The sailors were already occupying themselves bringing supplies from the hold to the galley. Much of the victuals had been ruined with all the water that had affected them, but everyone was in good spirits.

They lifted anchors at daybreak and as usual, at six thirty, the bell tolled for breakfast. Men and women got in line. In one corner of the *entrecoberta*, two colonists were throwing dice on one of the barrels for the items on their list of priorities when they received their homes upon their arrival in Brazil. They each had their own plans as to what they would do in the

Ponte Velha (over the Capibaribe River). Built in 1643, in Nassau's time, restored several times.

New World. They knew that the Aldeia dos Arrecifes was geographically located in the middle of wetlands, as in Holland.

They knew about Nassau's constructions, as well as the bridges that had to be built, for no matter where one went, one had to cross the Capibaribe River or the Beberibe River. They knew that, as in Holland, the sea accompanied the coastline of the city, and all wished to have their house facing the water, like the landowners in Holland.

Most of the crew and passengers were Calvinists, however, the Catholics also shared their dogmas with the only Jews on board, Sarah and Abraham, who were young and exuberant and pleasant to talk with.

When they discovered that the young man made maps and had knowledge about the stars, they hung about him. And Sarah, with all her talent and patience, entertained the women and children with her embroidery. Some of the young boys also followed Mr. Hondius, asking him to make hooks, lines, and sinkers and to teach them to fish. They fished with spears and hooks and lines depending on the size of fish they could hoist up to the deck and hold on to.

The children's favorite fish was the swordfish, which could reach five meters in length. It was great fun to catch one, especially to bring it on board. It was so exciting that many of the sailors would gather around, as a lot of strength was required to pull it out of the water. One had to wait for the fish to tire because it would take all the slack it was given, swimming back and forth, darting from one side to the other, flying out of the water and then submerging, fighting against the line around the ship until it had no further strength. Then it was brought up to the deck. The sailors were more than ready to prepare and savor the delicious fish. The most disputed part was the exotic saw itself, which was sought as a decoration in Holland. It was left to dry in the sun to lose its strong odor, and then stored to sell on their return home.

"Mr. Hondius, I think I have a bite," a 14-year-old boy was saying.

"Hold on tight and don't let it get away, my boy, especially this time of day when you can't see very well anymore."

"I don't know what it is; it's really pulling hard on the line."

At this point the Captain's voice was ringing out, trying to make himself heard by the nearer ships, starting to light the torches at the end of the day, and raising the white flag. This was the sign to the captains on the other vessels to immediately board his ship, and meant that there was an impasse for which a decision needed to be made, the order given directly by Banker himself, in writing—as if it were a memorandum.

In the blink of an eye, the leaders of all the ships that had survived the first storm went up to the Commander's quarters, where they conferenced for a few minutes. As they came out, the Captain gave further orders to his Chief Mate as he lowered the white flag.

"All passengers to your quarters. An enemy ship has been sighted. Position cannons. Sailors to your posts. Those that are ill, help unfurl the red flags, and cover the rails and the crow's nests with red cloth."

"But it's already getting dark, Captain," a sailor pointed out.

"Yes, but I want them to know that we will fight if necessary."

There was great fear as all rushed about in various directions. It was chaos itself. The sailors were trying to go down the steps to get what they needed, which was stored in a huge open barrel in the hold among the food supplies.

The other ships were following the same procedures. The sailors on the Zutphen, with their muskets in hands, were seeking the best positions for attack. Those in charge of the cannons were pushing them with their charges and heavy cannonballs, placing them in strategic positions. The cannons sat on a wooden platform with wheels, and were rolled and tied to the rails; they were extremely heavy. In a short period of time, with rapid preparations, the scene had become a wartime arena.

The Captain once more gave orders from the deck: "Keep the children in the entrecoberta," as several children were curiously sticking their heads out of their quarters to see what was going on.

All this confusion was caused by the sighting of a ship they didn't recognize. The Captain quickly went up to the deck to take a look, but not seeing it, ordered one of the sailors to go up to the crow's nest on the main mast. Frustrated, he asked for the direction it had been sighted, for there was a light mist, besides the darkness of night, making it practically impossible to see anything even a short distance away. He became even more alarmed when the sailor up in the crow's nest signaled there was nothing in sight—it was not possible to see the enemy ship.

"I don't know, Sir. I can't see it anymore. I did see it when I ran to tell you," an apprehensive sailor stated.

"I don't see anything moving either."

They remained alert until dawn.

Biscuits, crackers, sausages, butter, coffee, and tea were distributed to the passengers. The 'chow' routine had been broken and this was all they had to eat during the entire state of alert.

At eight, on the morning of the twentieth day after leaving Falmouth, the ghost ship was visible to all, for it was about six miles away. The Captain and his immediate subordinates were using their telescopes for a better look. Abruptly Mr. Hondius, also staring through his telescope, shouted: "It's a Spanish frigate."

The Captain ordered the route to be altered by two points to the SE, however, there was no response from the other ship. Without any warning, shots were heard coming from the pirate ship, and it was clearly headed towards the Zutphen. The fleet reacted with their cannons, hitting some of the Spanish pirates, who were, nonetheless, able to get to the Zutphen and board it. Even in a total state of alert, they had not been able to prevent the invasion. All of a sudden there were fifteen pirates running around the ship. When they removed the patches from their eyes and their red silk masks, it was apparent how mistreated they were—their teeth, their body odor—looking like wild beasts attacking their prey. They rushed to the *entrecoberta* where the passengers were and started to take their large trunks and boxes of jewelry.

They grabbed anything that was shiny, stashing it in their leather bags, hitting the passengers with the handles of their guns. Any child that ran around became a victim. The women and children couldn't stop screaming.

After a few hours, having checked all around the upper part of the ship looking for gold and money, which were not there, they went below to the hold and started taking the year's supply of food that was carefully stocked.

They were all running about with their bags, throwing everything into the pirate ship that was tied to the Zutphen. The Captain and his officers, up in the command quarters, were shooting at the pirates, who were not able to get back to them. They hit about six of them who were promptly tossed overboard by the sailors while the others were attempting to get back to their pirate boat.

The enemy's cannons were shooting at the other Dutch ships, trying to keep them at a distance.

The Zutphen was able to stand up to the attack, but two of the other ships were blown apart along with their sailors. Those that survived were divided up among the six remaining vessels.

The historic damage to the Zutphen was due to one of the cannons, which was hit and got loose from its ties, and thus rolled back and forth with the rocking of the ship, damaging the sides of the ship made of wood, therefore not strong enough to withstand the impact of the heavy iron structure. Yes, they were still in the middle of a hellish situation.

Captain Banker, Mr. Hondius, Abraham and Mr. Jodocus counted the possible dead, while trying to defend themselves from the loose cannon on deck. Finally, as the sun was setting, the badly damaged Spanish vessel disappeared, leaving in its wake great monetary ruin and loss of lives.

The following evening when the torches were lit and the sea continued choppy, the Captain spoke to the passengers for the first time since the battle: "We will care for the ill and pray for Divine Providence to give us strength to reach the Cape Verde Islands."

They were approximately twenty days away, depending on how the winds blew. Hearing their leader's voice, which felt like a soothing balm, the sailors and passengers began hugging and crying and trying to comfort each other, having as their motto the saga for a New World and their innate courage.

Several days went by on the high seas, the ships seemed like floating hospitals. Many had been hurt, some had died from infections, and others had had mental breakdowns, having to be kept in the hold.

It was very painful to watch some of the mothers say goodbye to their children as they were thrown into the sea. Some women had become widows and would not stop crying until they arrived at the Aldeia dos Arrecifes, where perhaps their relatives would comfort them.

The number of sailors had been drastically reduced, making for precarious conditions on the Zutphen as well as on the other ships. The food had to be rationed. Even moving around the ship was dangerous, for there were holes all round, including on the deck where the cannon had gotten loose and broken the rails before falling into the ocean. As there wasn't any wood available to fix the rails, Mr Hondius used some boards that had been shelves for food in the hold. Very creatively, he placed a hinge here, a nail there, a metal support where needed, temporarily replacing and repairing the damage to the walls of the mother ship, until they arrived in Pernambuco.

"Sarah, look what I have already embroidered," Maria shouted from the other side of the *entrecoberta*, trying to proudly show her what she had done.

"Come here, Maria, let me see."

Maria brought her embroidery cloth over, with her dream house she herself had drawn, outlined in backstitch with black thread, and inside that, had filled in the drawing with an attempt at cross-stitching.

"Look, Maria. Let's take out this line of stitches and do it again."

"But isn't it all right?"

"We're going to make it even better. Watch carefully what I am doing on my embroidery." And the two spent the rest of the day working on their projects together.

The sea was calm, offering tranquility to the passengers. Over in her corner, Sarah was showing Maria that one had to count the stitches two by two in the *talagarça*, so they would all be the same size.

"Now I see how you put all the stitches together that made such a pretty picture from far away, Sarah. I want my house to look pretty like that."

Sarah was very pleased at how sharp this little six-year-old child was, already wanting to learn a skill.

"Sarah," said Abraham, who came running, "I'm really worried about my ephemeris tables—I can't find them anywhere in our room."

"Do you need them right away? I'll help you look for them, but I didn't want to put my needles down just yet."

"It's that I think very soon now there's going to be a total eclipse of the moon in the Southern Hemisphere. I remember seeing the year 1640, but I don't recall the month. I'd really like to find out."

"Are you sure you're not mistaken? There was one in 1630 in the Southern Hemisphere."

"Yes, there was one then too."

"Now I'm curious too. Take a look in the leather bag where you keep some of your books."

So Abraham returned to their quarters.

Suddenly they heard the announcement from the deck: "Land ahoy! It's the Cape Verde Islands!"

And in a little over two hours they could see the northwestern coast of Africa and the Gambia River on the border of Senegal.

Mr. Hondius and Abraham were very busy recording the color of the waters, which varied from the coastline along Senegal all the way to the islands—ten in all, very green, with beaches having various colors. This was due not only to the depth of the waters, but also to the salt beds. Everyone was shouting with delight, for they knew they would be staying there until the ship was repaired.

Jodocus, as usual, was very excited and interrupted his conversation with the future colonists to say that he had already been there.

"This is a wonderful place! Excluding the Boa Vista Islands where there are many Portuguese, and the Island of Maio, which is frequented by the Spanish, the rest are fantastic."

"Where are we going to put down anchor?" one of the passengers asked.

"I don't know what the Captain will do this time. During our last trip to Recife, with the Prince, he stopped at the São Tiago Island, which I believe is the largest of all and is full of salt beds.

"Are there any lakes or rivers we can swim in?" one of the young boys asked.

"Yes, there are," Jodocus answered.

"I've been there too."

"Mr. Jodocus, don't let them interrupt you," said another passenger. "Let's continue talking about the São Jorge Fort in Recife."

"Yes. As I was saying, as soon as our men arrived in Olinda in 1630, they tried to take it during the early hours of the morning when night is at its calmest and darkest. Our soldiers knew about the fame and bravery of Captain Antonio de Lima, head of this fort.

"Did they succeed?"

"Well, on the first try, even with all of our courage, we lost because the ladders they took weren't long enough to reach the top of the walls of the fort, in Richshoffer. However, the second time around they captured the Captain, who was then forced to leave with all his soldiers. They were transported to the other side of the river, having to leave all their artillery and belongings behind, in the fort."

Questions rained down on Mr. Jodocus. When the sun was at its peak, Captain Banker gave new orders from the deck: "Tie up the ships. You are all free to leave. You should return for the evening meal and sleep on board. The ship will be refueled, resupplied, and repaired for a few days here."

Everyone stopped to listen to the Captain's orders and were very pleased to hear they could go ashore.

Mr. Jodocus tried to continue the conversation, saying that when the Dutch let down their anchor to look for supplies, they discovered that the Island of Maio was full of Spaniards, and exchanged not only shots but also taunted them, shouting, for example, *Spaniola cornudo* (horny Spaniard), and receiving in response, *Flamingo cornudo* (horny Fleming). There was much laughter as they listened to these stories.

"Actually, this isn't a laughing matter. You can't imagine how terrible it was at that time, and this feeling of nationalism stimulated both sides to fight against each other."

His audience slowly faded away until he realized he was speaking to himself.

They were all preparing to disembark. A few of the women with young children, though, did not feel comfortable leaving, and remained on the ship.

Seeing the ships, the inhabitants of the island soon filled the beaches. They consisted of whites, foreigners, harmless *degradados* (former prisoners facing severe punishments in their native land), Portuguese, and Jews peacefully welcoming the passengers and sailors. Many different languages were spoken in that little corner of the world, including Dutch. It was the Dutch who pointed the way to the fresh waters in a stream on the island.

What a celebration! Even the Captain mingled with everyone on land and was smiling broadly, saying, "I've been on this island several times before, and I'm always impressed by these natural salt beds that reach all the way into the sea."

"Sir, may we load up some salt?"

"Of course, and especially any fruit or vegetables you might find. The fish we catch can be salted."

"I'm going to try to get some pigeons which seem to be native to the island—I've never seen so many. And they're large and tame."

"All right."

"We might hunt some mountain goats also."

The sun set late—it was around eight when it began to get dark—on that 31st day of May. The passengers and some of the sailors were already on board; however, most of the latter had decided to stay out to drink and sleep on the sandy beach. They lit torches and spread their blankets out on the sand, for protection against the cool evening breeze that blew on the island.

They knew they would be there for at least a week because they needed to find wood, scrub down the ships, and if possible, get some rest.

On the main ship the meal schedule was once again changed. During the day while the sailors and carpenters worked on the ship, the passengers and crew were on the island eating goat meat, fresh vegetables, pure water, tea, and coffee. They also tried various types of fruit from the island, honey, and enjoyed other delicacies from the sea, baked and cooked, in holes in the sand on the beach.

Those were days filled with unforgettable exotic moments, a feeling of union with the luxuriant insular scenery. The fruit they enjoyed had been unknown to them, such as cashews and mangos. They loved the bananas and the native cherries similar to the *pitangas* they would taste on Brazilian lands in the New World.

"They were motivated by believing they were fighting in the name of the Lord. This idea or conception made it a just war" (in the presentation of the book Diario de um Soldado, written by Ricardio José da Costa Pinta Neto. Nossa Sra. da Piedade, October 1077).
Thus, somewhat frightened, but trusting the captain, the passengers tried to settle down, until they heard his voice once again from the deck: "The Lord is with us. Let us read from Psalms 107, verses 24-28.
According to custom, the sailors committed themselves to these prayers, which were frequent religious acts, especially on the warships.

O estímulo era dado no sentido de que guerreavam em nome do Senhor. Era uma idéia ou uma concepção de guerra justa" (na apresentação do livro Diario de um Soldado, *feita por Ricardio José da Costa Pinta Neto. Nossa Sra. da Piedade, outubro de 1077).*
E assim, meio assustados, porém confiantes no capitão, os passageiros tentavam se acomodar, até que se ouviu a sua voz outra vez do convés: – Até aqui nos ajudou o Senhor, leiamos o salmo 107, versículos de 24 a 28.
E como era de costume deles, os marujos se cometeram às correntes de orações daquele momento. Este ato religioso era freqüente, principalmente entre os navios de guerra.

The women spent their time washing clothes in fresh water. They had to work out in the burning hot sun, not having a way to protect themselves from it. Their children, however, bathed and dressed in long sleeved shirts and placed them in the shade under the trees. Now all cleaned up, they were very happy and would never forget those days. A few of them, though, did get so sunburned that they could not put on clothes.

They were so pleased to be on land. No one complained until one fine day, after everyone had turned in for the evening, the Captain issued new orders from the deck: "Today, June tenth, will be our last day on land. Tomorrow at daybreak we will raise anchors. I need everyone on board by the Angelus bell."

As soon as he had finished speaking he saw that the Den Ouwevaer Dutch ship was arriving on the island, with two small boats, trying to put down anchor.

"Notice the WIC flag," the Captain shouted. "It is one of ours. God is with us; it is one of ours," he repeated. "This is good—tomorrow we will try to exchange supplies with them."

Morning arrived with the beach full of sailors, and the Captain of the Den Ouwevaer, Claus Durcksen, came over to the Zutphen to speak with his old friend, Captain Banker. They had sailed from Curaçao and were loaded down with gold, sugar, pau-de-bacalhau (a strong-smelling wood), and water, which they had replenished at Cape Tiburon. The two Commanders visited for a few minutes and finally agreed to exchange supplies.

Captain Banker's fleet offered salted meat, and Captain Ducker, supplies such as manioc flour and lard. The best deal however was the pau-de-bacalhau, the wood they would use to repair the mother ship, for the bushes on the island had not been sufficient for this purpose. Even so they would have set sail had it not been for the arrival of the Den Ouwevaer.

The Captain also offered Banker some 1639 leaflets from Holland that had been given to him in Curaçao, and during a few hours they studied the inventory of the WIC's cargo that had been loaded and unloaded in the New World, for the WIC was on the verge of bankruptcy.

It was a long but pleasant day. The sailors were still working, carrying the supplies from the other ship through the hatchways to be stored in the hold. Around three in the afternoon, the passengers that had gone to shore were already forming a line in the sand on the beach, awaiting the orders to board the ship. The torches were about to be lit when the Captain announced that they would be remaining a little longer on the island to try to completely repair the ships with the recently arrived wood. So, on this wonderful day with a beautiful sunset, everyone's spirits soared to see the anchors dropped into the water again. They spent ten more days there until the Captain was satisfied that everything was in order for them to set sail for their destination.

They sailed along the coast until they rounded the island. Five days had passed since they had left Cape Verde, when the Captain announced the death of two children from dysentery and a sailor from scurvy (a disease caused by the lack of vitamin C). Those were inconsolable moments. As each of these difficult events reoccurred, there was more and more solidarity among those on the ship.

The following morning they crossed the Equator. The sailors couldn't let this event pass unnoticed, so they, as well as Abraham, jumped into the ocean, celebrating crossing the Line of the Equator. Their location was 7 degrees and 17. They were frolicking around enjoying themselves, when they saw a group of dolphins making pirouettes around the ships about a mile away . They responded gracefully to the sailors' whistles by performing a number of summersaults.

Mr. Hondius, who was on the deck, abruptly started warning everyone to get ready for a possible storm headed their way. The trip was like a Pandora's box, and this dance of the little dolphins was their sign to humans. Some of them decided to get their hooks and lines to see what they could catch—and someone actually caught a giant turtle. They were only able to get it on board after three sailors had jumped into the water and turned it upside down, keeping it from diving to the depths of the ocean with the hook in its mouth.

It was so exciting that everyone rushed over to look at the creature. It was large enough to carry a man on its back, so they lined up to ride it around the deck, until the chef arrived to take it to its final destination.

"Save the shell," a few sailors suggested, because they knew how to fashion it into combs and bracelets, which were prized in Europe.

Mr. Jodocus took care of feeding stories to the passengers, who were counting the days to sight land, in the midst of calm seas, winds blowing in a favorable direction, storms, and dreams about the things they wished to see and have.

"What finally happened with Captain Salvador Azevedo, Mr. Jodocus?" Abraham asked.

*Os jesuítas – repita-se – deram no século XVI valor exagerado ao menino inteligente... mas essa valorização artificial era conseguida sacrificando-se na criança sua meninice... e por meio de castigo e privações". (*Casa Grande e Senzala, *pag.74).*

"He was also imprisoned with his twenty-two soldiers, according to a captain that was there in 1630, who had made it through various battles and returned to Holland in 1636. He told me that the School of the Jesuits had an enormous number of orphan boys that the priests used for different types of favors, in exchange for teaching them the Tupi-Guarani and Latin languages. These children died young from all of the hard work forced on them. I was quite upset to hear these stories."

"So, these children were released when the Dutch arrived in Pernambuco in 1630?"

"I don't know if it was with our arrival. But you are a Jew!"

"When the Calvinists arrived, the slavery of the Indians was exchanged for that of the Blacks from Africa, 'utilized' mainly by the *senhores de engenho* in Pernambuco, who were, in the 16th century, mostly Jews and New Christians."

The ship continued on its voyage over an ocean containing surprises at every turn. All of those on board were full of hope and anxious to arrive. However, by now, the odor of the pau-de-bacalhau used to repair the damage caused by the pirates, was almost unbearable, and sometimes caused strange behavior. For example, from one minute to the next, the sailors would jump into the water and stay there until they could forget about the foul smell on the ship. The temperature of the water was warm and comfortable. Thus the days went by.

The men always got together to reexamine their lists of priorities, which they intended to fulfill upon arrival. They played dice for hours on end, thoroughly intent on establishing themselves in Pernambuco.

Captain Banker, Mr. Jodocus, and Mr. Hondius were always together discussing some issue. Sometimes they requested that Abraham join them; however, he always maintained a slight distance from him because he was Jewish. They would discuss the Company's economic situation, which they knew was not good, and sometimes, Mr. Jodocus, who was the storyteller and loved to kid around, slipped in a comment about the WIC's problems, raising their concerns.

"When you arrive, you won't have much in the way of opportunities, because the Prince has a system in place where the people of the land are elected as members of the chambers, the so-called escabinos, or rather the elite, his close friends. Those that rule the land are the Brazilians and Portuguese who are already there."

"How does it work, Jodocus?"

"I don't actually understand it very well, but I know they nominate the voters, who then choose several people, mainly the big local landowners, and then the Supreme Council appoints them. There's more to it. There are also escoltetos, the Prince's inspectors and magistrates, who preside over the chambers of the escabinos. This is not a small colony like the one in New Amsterdam in the Northern Hemisphere. In Brazil, the people already maintain a certain order and the King of Portugal is all powerful in the colony."

"Abraham, can you come here for a minute, please?" Sarah asked.

"Dear, it's not good for you to listen to this conversation of drunken men."

"That's not what it is. He isn't drunk right now. He just talks a lot, but I know that what he is saying is also of concern to him, and I think he is telling the truth."

Mr. Jodocus continued speaking to his audience, "We know that the Prince meets privately with the Brazilians and with a famous priest in the area, Padre Vieira, to discuss political issues on the new continent."

"Doesn't that put us in a bad position? I'm exchanging Holland for Brazilian land and have brought my whole family to this region of the New World, hoping to prosper and become wealthy."

"Don't give up, my friend. If I were you, I just wouldn't count on certain things. After the Portuguese set fire to a number of the *engenhos* in Pernambuco and surrounding areas, the Company's situation has deteriorated quite a bit. The demand for sugar in Europe is great and already we are not able to fulfill it, at least with the sugar from this land."

It was already the second part of August when they sighted the lands of Pernambuco. They were headed NW, nearly arriving in the port of Igarassu, when Captain Banker called Abraham and Mr. Hondius to his quarters. The Captain gave Abraham 400 florins in exchange for one of the maps he had made during the four months at sea, where he had also recorded the unexpected stops. Mr. Hondius handed Abraham the address of the office at the passo (the sugar warehouse) where he would be in charge of loading the goods for their final destination—Chile.

The passengers were excitedly gathering up their belongings. Of the original ten families, totaling fifty passengers, only thirty-nine remained, due to the difficulties experienced along the way: the storm, pirate attack, and illnesses.

Sarah's pregnancy was now apparent; she was already in her seventh month. Returning from his meeting with the Captain, Abraham joined her, as they heard the Captain's final orders.

When they arrived, there was a huge crowd awaiting them. Those on the ship tried to pick out their relatives. Those on land waved and shouted, looking for their family members.

Abraham shortly saw the Dias Fernandes Family. They had printed their name in very large easy-to-read letters on an empty sugar crate.

They came off the ship as they were accustomed to: one at a time, backwards, holding on to the rope and wood ladder that swayed back and forth with the movement of the waves.

The Captain addressed each passenger individually, shaking their hands before they left the ship.

Now only the cargo needed to be unloaded, so the boat moved slowly South to its anchorage, without any passengers. It sailed past Olinda and arrived in a large bay in front of the *Perriril*, (beside the old Forte de São Jorge, which later became the Forte de Santo Antônio dos Coqueiros, and is now the Forte do Buraco).

After the cargo was unloaded from the holds and the sailors were dismissed, Captain Banker went to the Palácio de Friburgo where he reported in to the Prince.

At the Port of Igarassu where the passengers had arrived, the meeting of the families was very emotional.

Obs. O destino era o Chile, mas ninguém cruzava pelo Pacífico, tentavam descer o Atlântico, voltando pela Argentina, através do Pacífico.

Obs. Their destination was Chile, but no one crossed the Pacific; they tried to go down via the Atlantic Ocean, rounding Argentina.

"It's so great to see you Abraham. Let me speak with your wife Sarah. Isn't she beautiful! And she's expecting? When is the baby due?"

"We think in October."

"That's wonderful. Come. Come. Let's go home. We made *matzo* soup for you. The people of the land are so nice; you'll see. We love it here, and so will you."

"Is it always this hot?"

"Yes, but you'll soon get used to it. What really matters is that there is a lot of fresh water here."

They were all laughing as they got up in the horse carriage. It was almost eleven o'clock and they soon discovered it would take them around four hours to get to the Camaragibe *engenho.*

"You know, Abraham, this trip reminds me of the one we took from Delft to Rotterdam with Mr. Jodocus and his son Pieter."

"Speaking of Mr. Jodocus, there he is, waving at us."

"David," Abraham said to his cousin who was leading the reigns, "can we go that way? I need to speak with a friend that came over with us, Mr. Jodocus."

"I thought you were going to leave without speaking with me," Mr. Jodocus told them.

"Never," Abraham said.

Sarah asked their cousin for the address where they would be staying, to invite Mr. Jodocus to visit them in their new home.

"Mr. Jodocus, this is my cousin Davizinho."

"It's a pleasure to meet you. I'm David. Sarah asked me to give you our address, and she has told me you know Recife very well."

"Well, not really, but I told Abraham I had heard about the Camaragibe *engenho*.

"And about its legends and ghost stories also? That makes it easier then. Why don't you come for my wedding, which will be on September 26? Remember, it's quite a ways from Recife. It will be on a Friday, a day before Rosh Hashanah, and we'll have a large celebration at the *engenho*."

"I'm not sure that I'll still be here. The Zutphen is going all the way to Chile this time, but I'll go if I can. And, you know, I already miss you! Either way, let's keep in touch. Whoever receives news first from Delft and everything we left behind, will let the other know, okay? And we will keep this our secret."

"We'll see you then. Goodbye."

From a carriage near them, Maria shouted Sarah's name very loudly to say goodbye, and Sarah answered, "Bye, Maria. I'm sure we'll see each other again. Keep on embroidering. Bye-bye."

The trip was quite uncomfortable because they were traveling on dirt roads full of holes. Sarah arrived tired and sore. This trip had been a battle in itself. However, when she had her first view of the manor house of the *engenho*, surrounded by royal palm trees, cashews and many other fruit trees, the Dondon river running behind the house marking the boundaries between this *engenho* and the neighboring one, São João da Varzea, she felt a myriad of emotions. Then she saw a large number of slaves busy in the moenda (mill), horses, cows, children, along with the smells of sugar and sugar cane juice. All of this had a wonderful effect on Sarah, marking a unique moment in her life.

She leaned her head on Abraham's shoulder and tears of joy welled up in her eyes. They both cried, moved by the experience.

It was without a doubt the best *engenho* in the colony, according to Jerônimo de Albuquerque (*Senhores de Engenho*, p. 128).

When they stepped down from the carriage, there was already a *preta* with orders to care for Sarah. She was to be her maid—her name was Luzia. She was practically the same age as Sarah, or at least she appeared to be twenty-some years old. She was very jovial, and as soon as she saw Sarah, she realized she was expecting. This made her even happier, and she excitedly told them that she loved caring for children, that she had 19 brothers and sisters, and had helped her mother raise several of them.

"That's enough, Luzia," Davizinho was saying. "This woman talks too much."

This was an entirely new situation for Sarah and Abraham. He was more introspective than Sarah, observing everything out of the corner of his eyes. He saw that Sarah was happy, had a contented look on her face, and was reacting positively to everything.

There were seven people standing at the front door of the manor house anxiously awaiting them. They were relatives on both Abraham's and Sarah's sides of the families, even distant cousins. Davizinho's brothers and sisters and parents were all descendents of Branca Dias and Diogo Fernandes. Branca Dias had arrived in Brazil from Vieira da Foz do Lima in Portugal with her husband Diogo Fernandes, who had received the fourth part of a sesmaria of Camaragibe in 1542, with all due rights including "water rights to the Caragibe River" (*Gente da Nação*, p. 127).

At dinner, the owners of the house, Senhor David and Dona Beatriz, sat at the head of the enormous table of *bois de pernambouc* with all of their children and Angela, David Filho's fiancée, sitting around them. It was a very pleasant event because Sarah and Abraham had a number of stories to tell, and everyone was very interested in what they had to say. The *mucamas* brought plate after plate of food on tin trays, until one of the *mucamas* whispered in Dona Beatriz' ear that Dona Umbelinda had arrived.

Dona Beatriz got up from the table and called Sarah to go with her to the other room.

There stood an elderly simply dressed black woman.

"Sarah, this is the midwife in the area. She delivered my babies."

Dona Umbelinda was a slave that had come from Africa in the last century and had ever since been a midwife. She was called practically twice per month to deliver a baby. She did not diagnose, but she did medicate. Observing Sarah's swollen feet she asked her to lie down and rest for half an hour at least twice during the day, and that she drink a cup of quebra-pedras tea daily, for proper functioning of her kidneys.

"What's that, Beatriz?"

"It's a well known herb in this area, and some people actually drink it to dissolve kidney stones or reduce swelling."

"Don't worry, child. Your mucama knows where to find such things."

Beatriz walked with them to Sarah's room so Dona Umbelinda could examine her more comfortably and calculate the day of birth. After checking Sarah, she announced: "I believe this child will be born in the first days of October and my guess is that it is a baby boy."

"How can you tell?" Sarah asked, in both wonderment and happiness.

"Your stomach is a little pointy and sticking out. Did you have a lot of nausea in the beginning?"

"Yes, quite a bit. I was on the ship, though, for four months. I had a lot of nausea at the beginning."

"Right. I'm fairly sure it is going to be a boy because your stomach is sticking out. That's it—pregnancy with a boy is tough," the elderly woman was saying quite authoritatively.

After Dona Umbelinda left, they laughed about the type of science that the black woman relied on, but they trusted and accepted her.

The two women continued talking, with Dona Beatriz saying, "I'm right in the midst of my son Davizinho's wedding plans."

"He told us he's getting married on September 26."

"Right, and that's just around the corner. We will have the celebration here at the *engenho* because his fiancée's family has only recently arrived in the colony, and they don't know many people yet. They're from Vila de Favaios in Lamego, Portugal.

"It's so fascinating—everyone here is from a different place. For example, we're from Antwerp in what is now Belgium. And what is interesting is that we all speak Portuguese.

"Come, Sarah, lets go visit with Angela. I know you met during dinner but didn't get the chance to talk much. You're almost the same age and are both from Portugal, so you have a lot in common. She is a wonderful person, and has many skills."

"Angela, I want to present you formally to Sarah."

"It's a pleasure, Dona Beatriz," Angela said politely, and looking at Sarah, added, "Sarah, I'm jealous of you with your baby."

"Listen to that. You'll soon be able to have a baby too, but you're very young."

"I'm already seventeen, and I hope to be so lucky. I love children, and Davizinho and I want to have a lot of them."

Dona Beatriz left to check on the rest of the family.

"Where do you live?"

"At an *engenho* near here, the Ipojuca *engenho*. I'm the daughter of Mateus da Costa.

"One of these days I would like to know how all these families arrived here, because our voyage was very difficult. I'll tell you more about it sometime."

"Come, Sarah. Come, Angela, let's go sit in the living room for a while.

Sarah, however, excused herself, saying she was exhausted and would like to go to her room.

"Of course," the other two women answered.

"I'll call Abraham so he can accompany you. He's probably very tired also."

Sarah and Abraham, feeling very well accepted by their relatives, bid everyone a good night. In their room, Abraham told her what he had decided to do with Senhor David. Tomorrow he was going to go with him to find out about the passo at the docks in the port of Aldeia dos Arrecifes.

"It sure is hot here, Sarah. I'm going to need to wash up again." He had washed before dinner, but he was feeling sticky again.

"The jar and basin are on the table in the bathroom."

"Aren't you hot?"

"Yes. I'm going to wash up too before I change. I have to call Luzia to bring more water.

As she was speaking, Luzia knocked on the door with the water.

The day at the *engenho* started early. At six o'clock people were already at their posts at the eito, the bagaceira, the moenda, and the manor house. The first shift was from six to nine in the morning, and the second from three to six or seven in the afternoon.

This was the only way the *senhores de engenho* had found to keep their slaves working for them: not having them work at the hottest time of the day with the sun burning their backs, furrowed by the whips of the overseers, the capitães do mato. There were great numbers of slaves. They were traded intensely on the coasts of Africa with Arab merchants, during the 17th century. When the blacks arrived here, however, they couldn't take the pressure of the overseers at the *engenhos* and ran away to the quilombos.

Inside the manor house, Sarah and Abraham were eating breakfast, which was without a doubt another new experience: generous servings of regional fruits, juices, and all kinds of roots, making it difficult to decide what to try first.

"Don't think too much about it and just take a little taste of everything," Dona Beatriz said as she approached the table. She sat down with them and explained all of the traditional food before them, one by one. "This is tapioca, made from manioc flour. Remember the fried macaxeira you had for dinner last night? Well, you make a type of batter with the starch from the root of the same family, manioc, and cook it in a skillet. It is almost like a tortilla. Then you fill it with shredded coconut. Or, you can put butter in it, which will melt. It is delicious."

"Mmm! It is delicious," Sarah said as she tasted it with a swallow of *erva-cidreira* tea.

"Mmm! I agree," Abraham added, who was especially enjoying the cheese.

There wasn't any bread because it was difficult to transport flour to the area.

They ate *beiju* and *broas*, which could be used like *emparedados* for cheese or whatever else they wanted to put between them.

Senhor David, ready to go, appeared in the dining room and called Abraham to accompany him to tend the horses. He was also in a hurry to take care of the inventory business with the Dutch at the passo.

"Yes, I'm ready," he said a little unenthusiastically, for he was not ready to leave the breakfast table yet.

The two left on horseback, wearing dark wide-brimmed hats and bombacha pants, leather whips in hand. They were the most authentic prototypes of the rural aristocracy in the colony.

Young Abraham observed how the *senhor de engenho* carried himself, arrogantly, which was something new to learn.

They rode their horses for about two hours until they reached the Ribeira Marinha dos Arrecifes, or Aldeia dos Arrecifes. The name had not yet been defined.

Senhor David made this trip once a week and Abraham already realized that he would be the one to do so now. During the ride he had the opportunity to

SUGAR MILL – Illustration from Historia Naturalis Brasiliae, Leiden, 1648.

imagine his future. He would be a respectable judge of the *bois de pernambouc* that came from the Camaragibe *engenho* to be sent to Europe, as well as in charge of storing and exporting the sugar, which was already in crates when it arrived at the port.

"Here we are!"

As they neared the Forte do Picão, the scenery looked like a human anthill. Abraham soon learned that besides being a work place, people also lived there, making him all the more curious to see where his office would be.

In the meantime, back at the *engenho*, the preparations for the wedding were going ahead full speed for it would be taking place very soon.

The maids were starching the embroidered tablecloths from Madeira, while the slaves worked outside the house, planting ornamental flowers around the native philodendrons, such as the yellow and orange flamboyant trees that provided shady niches for the decorative orchids in the garden. Dona Beatriz loved flowers, and everywhere she traveled she brought back some little plant for her garden.

"Hey, José, how are you shaping that tree?" one worker asked the other. The trees were still small and being trimmed in the shapes of animals, for example, birds and elephants, to decorate the area around the small tables that would be spread about.

Bois de Pernambouc = Pau Brasil (Brazil wood.)

The beiju made of manioc, took the place of the asmo or ázimo bread, was used by the Jews in Brazil since the XVI century.

Davizinho's family had planned a relatively small wedding. Those invited included the bride's and groom's families, the Rabbi, Senhor Asser Levi and family (best friends of the Dias Fernandes'), and other close friends from the synagogue. They expected around fifty people. It was to be a private celebration because of the religious aspect involved. Every effort was made to not publicize the Semitic ritual important to the family.

Sarah and Dona Beatriz kept busy teaching renda de bilro (lace making) and cross-stitching to the young girls in the area around the *engenho*, and there were quite a few.

Sarah, who was now quite large, couldn't sit for very long. Even so, they would get together two afternoons a week in one of the rooms of the manor house, that many years ago, since Branca Dias' time, had been designed for this purpose. Her ancestor, Dona Branca Dias, had become famous in the society of the 16th century for teaching homemaking skills and her embroidery. In those days the young girls already learned to embroider, sew, comb their hair with marrafas, braid their long hair, set a table for a banquet, and everything about personal hygiene and hygiene in the community. These young Jewish girls were alphabetized at home by their own parents, who did everything to maintain their tradition, and they also had further training in the synagogue on Saturdays, when they only spoke Hebrew.

The days passed by, and suddenly it was September 24.

Dona Beatriz, working alongside the slaves in the kitchen, never tired of preparing the fartes, a sugar and almond filling inside a dough made of flour (brought over from Europe especially for the wedding), eggs, and milk. Dona Beatriz, very creatively, substituted the filling in the original recipe for chopped cashew nuts or shredded coconut. She also prepared the little cheese balls that would be covered with delicious caramelized sugar syrup, thus continuing the candy-making tradition in Pernambuco.

It was actually a hermetic institution, which consequently made the Aldeia dos Arrecifes and surrounding sugar region into one great family. The objective was to avoid miscegenation of adventurers or *mulatos* and *mulatas* with the whites.

It was very rare for a *mulatos* to marry into a family and ascend socially, but a few cases have been recorded. They became part of the aristocracy of Pernambuco, and were good noblemen like their in-laws, according to Gilberto Freyre in *Casa-Grande & Senzala*.

Their closest friends from the synagogue were invited a month before the wedding. Some of them brought their presents immediately. A fabric businessman, who was also a tailor, made Davizinho's outfit for the wedding, having to make several trips to the Antonio Vaz residential area for fittings until it was right.

The bride was prepared by her mother and Dona Beatriz, who between themselves at the two *engenhos*, sewed the dress by hand. It was a beautiful dress made of white silk, all embroidered, trimmed with lace around the cuffs, and with a princess collar.

The ceremony was set for six in the evening, but the guests began arriving much earlier in their carriages, carts, and on horseback. Senhor David gave orders to stop the moendas and for the workday to end at five, which was adhered to. The slaves that would be helping at the wedding were well dressed: the women in their colorful long silk skirts, flowers in their hair, and adorned with many bracelets and necklaces; the men wearing black bombacha pants, and white shirts with white organza collars. They were all well trained, for they participated in the feasts for the saints, which the New Christians celebrated for those from the outside. The family also followed the Catholic liturgy and celebrations, to avoid problems with the inquisition.

New Christians tried, on one hand, to attract as little attention as possible from the persecutors, and on the other, to bring happiness to the colonists who loved to celebrate special days.

They called the feasts of circumcision, for example, feasts of baptism, dividing them into two parts.

On the day of the wedding ceremony, the small tables were spread on the grass in the shape of a half moon, within a radius of about fifty meters. The wedding table to be used for the ritual of the ceremony was placed in the center, and in front of the half moon of chairs, where all the guests sat facing forward.

When the bride and groom arrived, they stood in front of the table that was in the center of this half circle of tables. The Rabbi faced not only the bride and groom but also all of the others.

Davizinho, 20 years old, was all in white in his kítel, and Angela wore her white wedding dress and a tiara of Angelica emitting a wonderful aroma on her head. The two stood before the Rabbi, under the huppah, a canopy of white silk. The Rabbi was from the synagogue on the Rua dos Judeus, which had been founded in 1637. The *Kidushin* ceremony was taking place on the seventh day, September 26. After the sermon, the vows, and the further exhortations, the Rabbi, with the wine and cups to his right, and the halla, the cake made of honey to his left, according to tradition, took the cup of wine and placed it under the groom's right foot; Davizinho mashed it, while everyone shouted, wishing the bridegrooms *mazaltov*, good luck.

After the blessing, the newlyweds left, turning their backs to the Rabbi and facing the guests, who followed them out in an orderly fashion, two by two.

The dance began shortly in the midst of hugs, kisses, crying, and much happiness. In the dance circle, where they sang and played Jewish songs, two flute players and a fife player sat. The high point of the dance only occurred when the newlyweds were lifted up in two separate chairs in the center of this circle. In the meantime, the tin trays, laden with a variety of sweets and finger food were being offered to all. There was also no lack of drinks.

This was one of those ingratiating days for the Jewish Nation.

"Abraham, Mr. Jodocus didn't make it," Sarah said.

"I expected he wouldn't, dear, first because when the groom-to-be was presented to him, they didn't get to talk very long, and, he probably knew that the families at this *engenho* ever since it was acquired have been New Christians, which is suspect among Christians.

"Remember when he said that he had friends at the synagogue on the Rua dos Judeus?"

"Yes, I do. Also, he might have had to continue on his voyage."

"I'll find out about this second theory on Monday when I'm at the Passo. I'm also curious to know if the Zutphen is still around or if it has already been repaired."

"Sarah, when do you think the baby will come?" some of the women asked.

"In the second week of October, I think. You know, I can hardly stand to wait anymore. Is it usually so uncomfortable to be expecting?"

"Yes," they all answered in chorus. "But after the baby is born you'll feel it was all worth it, and soon you'll want another one."

"I hope so. It's just that I have a lot of pain all the time on my right side, as if something is pushing against my ribs."

"That must be awful," an elderly woman who had had ten children remarked. "You should see a doctor so he can check your lungs."

"Do you think it could be a lung problem?"

"I can't really say, Sarah, but the place you are pointing to could be your lungs."

"Did you hear that, Abraham?"

"Yes, dear, and I'm going to follow your advice. We'll take care of it right away."

"Look how beautiful Angela is, so young, she doesn't even look seventeen. I still don't know where their house is."

"Oh, it's a two-story house in Apipucos, a present from her father. I'll take you there sometime. I saw it when I was with David helping move Davizinho's things in. It's very pretty. The land right beside theirs has a famous stream on it, the Riacho da Prata, and on the way we have to go by the Casa Forte *engenho* that belonged to Dona Ana Paes.

"Come on, everyone. Let's go to the *hallá*," Dona Beatriz said, trying to get the attention of those guests who didn't want to stop dancing and singing in the circle.

"Wasn't it a wonderful celebration, Sarah?" Abraham asked as they walked hand in hand towards their room. Sarah was quite big and it was late at night.

They had promised Dona Beatriz, at her prompting, that they would remain at the *engenho* until the baby arrived.

"I've never been to a wedding this size."

"I also think that if it had been in Europe, our family wouldn't have done it in this fashion."

"Yes, here there is an abundance of everything. Even the slaves give their *senhores* an air of feudal sovereignty."

"The title *senhor de engenho* is vary valuable and bestows status, which is why anyone with possessions arriving here wishes to have the title."

"I understand it's valuable, but I'm satisfied with the work you are doing at the Passo. Do you think things will develop well for you there? We are planning on having a large family."

"I believe so. The rapid growth in the city contributes to what I'm doing. A lot of warehouses and other storage areas are being built on the docks for the huge numbers of crates arriving daily from the *engenhos* in the region. The area is also too small to store the basic goods, arriving from other countries, for the local population. I've been observing all these details related to the growth of the city, and I think what I'd really like to do is be an inspector at the docks. It's a great position. That's why I've decided I'm going to try to become a member of the Council of the Escabinos. Tomorrow at the synagogue I'm going to speak with one of the members of the chamber that I know. Then, someday I will be a government inspector at the sugar passo. There are a lot of jobs there and that's where I want to work. Maybe in the future we could have a store, Sarah."

"Yes, yes." Sarah was already asleep.

Two weeks later Dona Beatriz was urgently called from her embroidery room to take Sarah to the clinic in the Aldeia dos Arrecifes, where Abraham wanted the baby to be born because he already knew the place. The carriage was prepared and they set off. Sarah, however, began feeling too uncomfortable even before leaving the lands of the *engenho*. Quickly they changed their plan, deciding to return to the *engenho* and call Dona Umbelinda, who was brought on the fastest horse in the area. Less than two hours later, the cry of a beautiful baby could be heard. They named him Adam.

Sarah and Abraham remained at the *engenho* for two more months, until, in 1640, Abraham was able to purchase his two-story home in the beautiful highly desirable area of Apipucos, sought after by the wealthy families of the day.

All of their relatives helped them to move, taking with them Luzia, Sarah's nursemaid, and two other slaves for domestic help. Abraham continued working at the passo as a private inspector of the merchandise of the Camaragibe *engenho*. Senhor David found him to be a dynamic young man, and was the only person he really trusted. In 1642 Abraham was invited by a friend at the synagogue to work as a partner in a purchasing warehouse. He accepted the proposal and entered the partnership with 49% of the capital. Best of all though was his job with cousin David at the passo, where from that time on, he was able to negotiate a better work schedule: two hours per day instead of two days per week. He had his house, carriage, and everything he really needed. Times were becoming less and less difficult.

Sarah was about ready to give birth to their second child. Her embroidery, sewing, and homemaking skills classes she taught at home were full. She, as well as Dona Beatriz, had set aside a space full of tables and chairs for their students. The more people heard about their teachings on domestic skills, the greater was the demand for the classes.

Sarah had kept busy since arriving in Recife, even with her frail health and low level of energy. She still complained about pains in her ribs on her right side. No one had been able to find the cause of the pain, though, because after she gave birth it disappeared and everything was fine. She was very diligent and dedicated to everything she did, not trusting the slaves to do certain things.

Abraham was already importing foodstuff from Europe: flour, wine, spices from India, and silk for the select clientele in the old Cidade Maurícia. However, he still dreamed of receiving an invitation to become a member of the local Council of the Escabinos.

As time went by, the family became larger with the birth of the couple's fourth child, whom they named Branca. The oldest, Adam, was ready to be schooled, so his mother taught him at home, but on Saturdays the young boy was schooled at the synagogue. He was a bright and gentle child.

In this same year, 1646, Branca, a late child, ended up bringing them much luck. Abraham was finally appointed a member on the Council of the Escabinos. He was well known and liked in the community and was accepted to the Council during the same period it had become controversial in Europe. The older members considered Abraham very diplomatic and expected a lot from him, especially to be levelheaded during strong discussions, calming down those that became too exalted. Nassau, having disbanded the Chamber and the Forum in Olinda, transferring all to Olinda, affected the political structure of the WIC, which wanted a Dutch monopoly in everything and for everything in its dichotomous government.

Most members of the Council were successful local businessmen, *engenho* owners, Portuguese, Jews, and Dutch.

The Brazilians thought Nassau was too liberal. It is known that the Prince had a friendly relationship with those of the land, until he returned to Holland in 1644. He was constantly in contact with the Marques de Montalvão, who had been helping the Prince since 1640, during the critical period of transition and instability between the current Dutch government and the retaking of the government by the Portuguese.

It had not been easy, however, especially in 1644, when Dom John IV gave approval for the insurrection of Pernambuco against them.

Nassau had already been expecting a rebellion because of the social health of the community—huge debts, semi-freedom in religious expression while the inquisition continued making its visits, besides the problems caused by the cultural aversion of the Dutch with those of the land, which had become unbearable. Few, actually very few, intermarried in this 30-year period. An example of one who did was Senhor De Witt, who wed Ana Paes, and ended up in a bad situation for having taken his wife's side "approaching the insurgents concerning the possibility of their remaining in the land if the Portuguese dominion was reestablished." (*Rev. Continente*/Year II, number 16, April 2002, p. 62, by Evaldo Cabral de Mello). Mr. de Witt had been

Captain of Nassau's Guards and was forced to return to Holland as a prisoner.

When Nassau left in 1644, Recife, having lost its great supporter, became an 'orphan.' The battles against the Dutch continued until 1654, when many had returned to the Old Continent. A new wave of immigrants, Jews and Dutch, then began a new saga, this time in the New World, in the Caribbean Islands, such as Barbados an Curaçao, and to the north where a Dutch Colony had been developing in New Amsterdam since 1614.

There was much confusion in the lands of Pernambuco and once again there would be the need to leave the dreams behind. The saga of the instability of a race had a high cost.

When the Portuguese retook control of the Brazilian lands in 1654, the Jews in Pernambuco were given a choice: to leave within three months, or to remain and be treated as the Jews in Portugal, having to convert publicly or submit to the tribunes of the inquisition, *A Fenix ou o Eterno Retorno.*

In reality, it was of interest to the Portuguese crown to have these Jews in their domains, preferably in Lisbon, in their royal courts.

The royal vaults were empty, after all. There was no other reason for sending the seventeen ships to the Porto dos Arrecifes. Even though it might be a convenient or comfortable destination, not everyone wished to go there, although a good number did agree to go.

In a short period of time, Abraham was able to sell their two-story house for a small amount of money behind closed doors to some Portuguese relatives who had been living in the area for several years, and were

New Christians, following mainly the Catholic religious practices.

He had discovered through his contacts in the import-export transactions that an English ship, the Valk would be coming through the Aldeia dos Arrecifes at the beginning of the year, and he started to make plans with his closer friends, even knowing that this wasn't the most appropriate time for Sarah to travel. She was quite debilitated, coughing a lot and feeling strong pains in her lungs, as if she had tuberculosis.

Several days later the friends met again, and formed a group of twenty-three people who would leave together on this ship and head to the Northern Hemisphere of the New World.

Persecution of the Jews is a cruel reality. The Sephardim, even having suffered great hardships, contributed greatly to the Brazilian culture, especially in northeastern Brazil.
They became and continue to be prominent in various fields, such as medicine, physics, the arts, and literature.

(Author's Note)

Among them was Mr. Asser Levy, an important businessman on the Antônio Vaz island, his wife and two children; Mr. Abraham Israel, his wife and two grown children; Sarah, Abraham, and their four children, ages fourteen, twelve, ten, and eight; Mr. David Israel, brother of Abraham Israel, his wife, and three children; and Mose Lumbroso, wife, and two children.

On the day the ship was to leave, the twenty-three boarded the Valk and headed for New Amsterdam. They had already paid for their trip and had brought along and loaded up all of their belongings. It had been fourteen years since the Dias Fernandes' had gone on a voyage. This was the first trip, however, for their children, who were very excited about the idea of traveling on a ship, even though the farewells had been difficult.

The story of the Sephardic community, based on reports appearing from the 17th century on, and according to Maria Antonia Bel Bravo, who was "the mother of the Judeo-Spanish-Portuguese Diaspora in the West," the first members of the nation to settle there at the end of the XVI century, arrived as Portuguese Catholics. (*Diaspora Sefardi*, p. 62)

It is also known that a large number of them came from Antwerp, a port city in current Belgium. *Studia Rosenthalia*, 5 (1970, pp. 25-42), by E. M. Koen, presents a very interesting explanation about the history of the Portuguese, the greatest contributors to the growth of Amsterdam up to 1620.

"Ir à prancha: forma de execução aplicada aos condenados que eram jogados ao Mar"

The twenty-three Sephardim, who left the Aldeia dos Arrecifes in 1654 heading for New Amsterdam, were of the same lineage as those who first left Spain and Portugal in 1492.

This story is told by Saul Levi Mortera in the manuscript studied by many researchers *Providencia de Dios com Israel* (1660. p. 58), and can be found at the Bodleiana library in Oxford, the Ets Haim D. Montezinos bookstore in Amsterdam, and the Stats-und Universitat in Hamburg.

Another written record, by Jehudad Machabeu, 1663, also recounts the history of this nation; the original edition is at the Oxford library (*A Fenix ou o Eterno Retorno*).

Everything was going wonderfully. There were only a few passengers and they all got along well. Those who knew English could communicate with each other, and those that spoke Yiddish kept more to themselves.

The sea had been rough for a few days, but as they advanced north it became calmer, although the sun was very hot. It was a typical voyage: crew and passengers had the opportunity to fish, the activity that everyone participated in during these anxious times.

As usual, Sarah was busy helping the children in her group read their books. There were thirteen children.

When they passed over the Equator, they celebrated as Sarah and Abraham and all the other Sephardim who had crossed the ocean from Europe to the New World had already celebrated.

Many took the opportunity to jump into the sea, as was the custom, and they celebrated with wine and *aguardente* (an acoholic beverage made from sugar cane). The crew was very enthusiastic, for the sailors were now on their way back to England and continuously counting the days. They were accustomed to this kind of voyage to the New World and this time there had not been any problems.

For several days they sailed by various islands in the Caribbean.

Suddenly, when they were nearing Cuba, a Spanish frigate attacked their ship and took it over. Life then became terrible for the group of twenty-three. The pirates wanted the passengers' jewelry, money, and all the valuables they possessed. Anyone refusing to cooperate with them was threatened: if a man, to walk the plank, and if a woman, to be handed over to the inquisitors at one of the Spanish administrative sectors on those islands.

Finding the booty very small, the captain of the pirate ship freed the Valk in exchange for some gold. However, he took all of the passengers as prisoners to his boat after relieving them of all their possessions.

They followed the coast around Cape Santo Antonio without going ashore, until they reached Cuba with their prey. The pirate leader immediately negotiated the prisoners with the Spaniards on the island, in exchange for supplies for their ship.

The days were interminable for the twenty-three. They were prisoners of the Spanish, barely surviving on their small portions of food while performing heavy labor.

As if a gift from the heavens, a ship on its way to New Amsterdam came into port at Cape Santo Antonio.

It was the Sainte Cathérine, a French ship, full of sailors who knew the coast of Brazil and the islands between the two Hemispheres very well. Its Captain, Monsieur Jacques Lacrois, was familiar with the coast of Pernambuco, and had become acquainted with many people from the Cidade Maurícia as he traveled his route from Africa, Europe, and the New World. Seeing the Jewish prisoners, he immediately began to negotiate their freedom. Captain Lacrois knew the island of Pavônia (Fernando de Noronha) very well, where he always stopped to rest and fish, while the French fort was being built. From there he would go on to Recife, taking imported items to the merchants. He shortly recognized Abraham and the other old Jews, residents at the Porto dos Arrecifes. Some of them also recognized the Gaelic navigator.

The twenty-three were, however, taken straight away to another area set aside by the town for those who were disruptive or committed crimes in the community.

Peter Stuyvesant, governor at the time, was very strict. He was averse to Jews, but the arrival of these twenty-three was different, for he already knew their profiles: he had received a written appeal from the commissioner of the WIC, who had worked with him in Pavônia when he was the WIC's commanding commissioner on that island of Pernambuco before going to Curaçao, Barbados and New Amsterdam.

The appeal emphasized the importance of these twenty-three Jews headed to the Northern Hemisphere aboard the Valk and not in Portuguese ships. It also highlighted the fact that they had been pillars in the Dutch colony since 1624, and that several of them were descendents of those residing in the Pernambuco capitancy in the 16th century before the WIC arrived in Brazil. They were actually the right hands of the Dutch (*A Fenix ou o Eterno Retorno*) as far as the sugar industry was concerned, having the know-how they had brought with them from the Azores Islands. Even more important was that they had invested a lot of money in the WIC and did not wish to lose it, for they could take their knowledge and efforts to New Amsterdam.

After much negotiating, Stuyvesant had to give in to his superiors.

This was how the Sephardim came to establish the first Jewish community in the New World, in New Amsterdam.

Stuyvesant gave them the privilege to practice their religion when they became citizens in 1657 (Gotham, by Burrows), at which point they constructed the historical synagogue Shearith Israel in current New York.

Ilha de Pavônia, name given to the island for its having been leased, at the time of the Dutch conquest, to a director of the WIC, Michiel de Pauw. Currently the Ilha de Fernando de Noronha.

Everything was proceeding very well and their businesses were flourishing.

Ashkenazim Jews began to arrive from Germany, joined them and all worked in harmony.

Only Sarah was not able to participate in the town's development. She was getting more ill day by day, and in 1656 she finally passed away. The others found comfort in that they were able to lay her to rest in the cemetery they had struggled so hard to obtain—they now had a cemetery.

A few days before she passed away, the Jewish community had united to promote a "community action" effort, the first of the Sephardim in New Amsterdam, pushing for their own cemetery, which was finally given to them by Stuyvesant (Jewish Landmarks in New York, an Informal History Guide, by Bernard Posta & Lionel Kappman. Hill & Wang, NY, 1964, p. 18).

MONOGRAM – Engraving reproduced in the book "De geschiedenis van de WIC". Walburg Pers, Zutphen, 1994

Sarah was then the first person to be buried in this little hook of land. Abraham soon recovered from his loss, and established the type of business he had had in the Cidade Maurícia, in Brazil.

A few years after Sarah's death, their oldest son, Adam, who also worked with his father, got married. His sister continued teaching the virginal at home.

Towards the end of her life, when she was quite elderly, she played in the 1730 inaugural commemorations of the Shearith Israel, the first synagogue in New Amsterdam. She had married and had a large number of children.

Sarah and Abraham's other two children returned to their parents' land where they married cousins in Antwerp.

New Amsterdam was now overpopulated and had especially a great number of Blacks who had started to arrive from Curaçao, the other Dutch colony in the New World (New York the Centennial Years 1676-1976. Ed. by Milton M. Klein. Kennitak Press, Port Washington, NY, 1976).

In 1664, Stuyvesant gave in to the English and in 1667, the city of New Amsterdam, after many meetings and decisions, was exchanged for Dutch Guyana, currently the Republic of Suriname.

The WIC had found it best to let the English have New Amsterdam, for they still believed in the sugar "drug."

Mose Lumbroso, and David and Abraham Israel, also became successful in their businesses.

Asser Levi set up one of the first business partnerships between Jews and non-Jews—a meat market.

"Application by Asser Levi for permission to build a slaughterhouse, New York, January 8, 1677-8. Partnership confirmed, October 8, 1678." (Herbert L. Osgood, ed. Minutes of the Common Council of the City of New York, 1675-1776, New York, 1905, I, 67-68)

The four surviving Sephardic Jews from Recife, plus Abraham Paz, had been the founders of the first synagogue in South America, in the old port area of Recife, the Kahal Zur Israel, where the historical archives of the Jewish Cultural Center in Pernambuco are located.

First Synagogue of the Americas
Rua do Bom Jesus—Old Rua dos Judeus
Recife—Pernambuco—Brazil

Chapter – Reality

Sarah Herckmann, after losing her husband John Herckmann, who was also of Dutch descent, never remarried. They had been so much in love. They met in the 1960s at New York University where they were both Journalism undergraduates, and then they continued into Master's Degree programs together.

Everything had been going perfectly: the two worked at different newspapers. She maintained a professional career at The Day and then tended to household duties, especially taking care of little Benjamin.

John was then drafted to go to war in Vietnam. And as everybody knows, and contrary to conventional wisdom and the predictions by Henry Kissinger regarding how a loss in Vietnam would cause all of Southwest Asia to fall, like dominoes, into Communist hands for all the world to see. We did lose, and the fall never happened. Nor did Sarah ever see her beloved John again.

Years later, Jacob became her good friend. He filled a certain intellectual emptiness in Sarah. He was well read and was extremely interested in Brazilian culture, which they discussed many times over the phone, almost always talking about their common ancestors.

Nassau, in the Northern as well as the Southern Hemisphere, brought the saga of the Dutch in the New World to a full circle. The Dutch had established themselves in both Hemispheres—for at least 30 years in Brazil, and a little more in New Amsterdam—maintaining their hegemony in both.

William of Orange Nassau, The Silent, then "stadhouder" of Holland, Zeeland, and Utrecht.

In 1540, the name Nassau was used to christen Fort Nassau in North America by Hendrick Christiaensen, an early pioneer. This fort had been abandoned by the French, who years before had visited this area near the city of Albany, north of the current state of New York.

Christiaensen decided upon this name in honor of Prince William.

New Amsterdam is a very interesting case. It became more prominent and more contentious after Willem Kieft, the fifth governor, arrived there in 1638 on the ship Haring. He began his government implementing drastic measures that devastated the lives of the newly-arrived, hopeful Dutch colonists. In an atmosphere of terror, he controlled the inhabitants of Staten Island, Manhattan Island, Long Island, and Governor's Island by going up and down the Hudson and East Rivers with his henchmen. He set up absurd *Artkelbrief* rules and regulations for the new colony. Perhaps they were an alibi to protect him from future investigations of his atrocities, knowing that sooner or later he would come before a court in Holland for his governmental acts in the colony.

Among many atrocities, he gathered military personnel and cartographers he had brought with him, and ordered them to locate all of the Indian tribes in the region. After organizing the expeditions according to his plan to conquer the land, he began to exterminate the Indian tribes one by one. This policy caused a great revolt among the natives of diverse tribes, which included the Mohawks, Mohicans, Iroquois, and mainly the Paumanacke of Long Island. They retaliated by attacking and killing innocent colonists. Even though these Indians were at a disadvantage, having only rudimentary weapons, they were able to destroy everything that had been built since 1626, that is, all construction since the arrival of first colonists who had settled around Fort Amsterdam and south Manhattan Island.

Before Kieft, in 1613, Adriaen Block called himself the Dutch governor of America. In 1624, Cornelis Jacobse May was designated the first director of the Province of New Amsterdam, and in 1625, Willen Verlust followed Cornelis as the second director of New Amsterdam. Peter Minuit became the third governor in 1626, and then before Kieft, in 1633, Wouter van Twiller became the fourth governor.

In Kieft's time, the city developed, in a manner of speaking. Breweries were built, tobacco was produced, and corruption thrived. The WIC sold what the breweries produced and imported wine. This led to the founding of the first distillery on Staten Island. A street was named "Brower Straet" (Bowery Street) in honor of the activity of the breweries. The negative side to this story could not be covered up, however, and conflicts arose. The resulting thievery, adultery, and death occurred constantly.

The population grew rapidly. There were many more men than women, because the WIC was not concerned about housing developments. Kieft, meanwhile, was preoccupied with the conquest of more land. In 1638, for example, Andries Hudde, who had come over with him, acquired what is now Harlem, a piece of land north of New Amsterdam.

Hudde was a forerunner of agrarian reform in North America. His method was to lease a piece of land for a 10-year period from the governor, after which time he would have the first chance to purchase it. In British law this is called quit rent. He would then pay for the land over time, thus fulfilling his debt to the WIC.

Kieft, very enthusiastic about his conquests, decided to establish outside the fort, the First Annual Cattle Fair. Products such as wheat, tobacco and meat were brought by inhabitants from the other side of the East River, now Brooklyn.

Still, these were years of terror under Kieft's government, and the repercussions of his atrocities ultimately caused his demise.

Even though there was all this euphoria in the colony, the loss of the WIC's hegemony was already apparent. The arrival of immigrants from many different regions, the French, Swiss, Africans, Germans, and Belgians—who arrived without any authorization and settled on Long Island, made it apparent the Company did not have the capacity to preserve the colony, maintain order, or enforce its laws.

By 1644, there was total chaos (notes Burrows in *Gotham*); everywhere it looked, the WIC saw that it was losing ground. In the Southern Hemisphere, the Portuguese were seeking to take back their largest colony, Brazil. Prince Mauritius van Nassau had left the New

World in this same year. The WIC had huge debts at this point, and in a final attempt to maintain order it decided to concentrate its efforts on New Amsterdam, believing that if it could hold on there, it might be able to regain its hold in Brazil; but on the other hand, if it did lose Brazil eventually, New Amsterdam would remain its last possession in the New World.

Not even the Church could keep the peace. Its mission was to implement standards of behavior, but in New Amsterdam, it was far from accomplishing this goal.

It did not have the power.

It had been in place since 1624, when Pastor Bastien Jansz, a few Friars from several orders, and Jesuits arriving with Father Isaac Jogues, established a good trade relationship with the natives.

Their most important project was the preparation and persuasion to purchase the island of Manhattan. This occurred in 1626, when Peter Minuit, from Westphalia, was able to come to a peaceful agreement with the Indians to purchase the island, or rather 22 acres, for 60 guilders, which today would be the equivalent of $24.00.

Introducing Minuit to Indians donors, the Church, more specifically Father Isaac Jogues, was able to commence bartering between Minuit and the Indians, which culminated in the greatest business transaction in Dutch history. For the WIC, this was the best deal ever reported. Father Isaac Jogues, who was also one of the pioneers in New York, left many reports and documents of the Company of Jesus, among other things about the development of Manhattan after its acquisition.

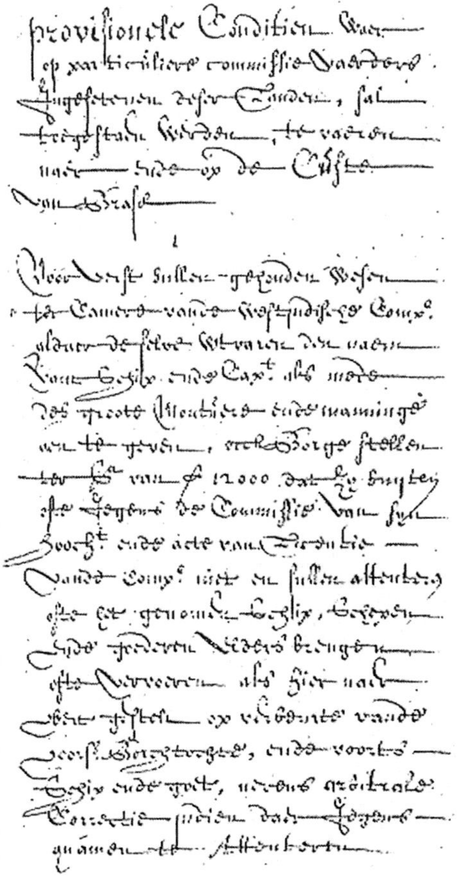

According to Jogues, New Amsterdam in 1640 already had a population of 7,000 and a variety of eighteen different languages. This all took place during Kieft's era, when although afraid, these European missionaries loved this land and repeatedly compared it to southern France where the perfume from the flowers filled the air.

It was thought by many that this land was marvelous, "a terrestrial Canaan," the Dutch poet Jacob Steendam said.

Its inhabitants were the subject of many a discourse and the missionaries vehemently defended the healthy natives. A famous appraisal by Jasper Danckaerts reads: "there are among them no simpletons, lunatics or madmen as among us" (Gotham).

The colonizers knew that by using psychology they could get everything they wanted from the natives without using force, and they stated that they, the Lenape tribe, owned the portion of land called Mannahata, which means "land of mountains."

The first church in Manhattan, according to the records, appeared in 1638 on Pearl Street. The Rev. Evardus Bogardus, the second offical in the province, delivered the sermons. He was considered to be the power behind the power at that time, having the ability to manipulate the three segments in the community: the governor, the colonists, and the Indians. (See *A Brief History of New York*, by George J. Lankevich & Howard B. Furer, ed. Port Washington, NY: National University Publications Associate Faculty Press Inc.)

This was, however, a very tumultuous period. (See *An Album of New Netherland*, by Dillard.) Even in the midst of all the immorality and promiscuity recorded at that time, 16th century Dutch women were well educated, culturally prepared, protected by the laws of their country, and more prominent than men. They exercised important positions within the community. The boys as well as the girls studied in coed schools, where they chose their own professions. The only difference being that the girls also received training for homemaking along with preparation for their careers.

As for religious freedom and tolerance, it did not exist, neither in New Holland in Brazil, nor in New Amsterdam. In Northeast America, the Dutch Protestant Church predominated, for example, protecting and controlling the governors. Whenever the government officials were notified of a religious act or conduct that went against the interest of the *senhores* in the region, they would penalize those involved in such a manner as to be an example to others, under the precept that they had broken religious laws.

VRYHEDEN

T'AMSTELREDAM

Only with the arrival of the Jews, Catholics, and Quakers, were laws implemented that protected and gave freedom to all the religions and sects, establishing separation between the government and freedom of thought.

In northeastern Brazil, during this period (1630-1654), the situation was somewhat different, for when the Dutch arrived, there was already a colony in place, consisting of different groups, and ruled by the royal orders from the courts of Lisbon.

The impact of this situation, this way of life in Brazil created a Dutch identity more ontological than social. They didn't have any reference points, for example, not even the word "chaos" fit. Integration was very difficult. The relationship between the invaders, who considered themselves the owners of Brazil, became more and more complicated, from a social as well as a political point of view. When the Dutch wanted to dominate, they did not mix with the Blacks or the Indians, as the Portuguese did, which caused much antagonism.

The result being that the existing culture clashed with the Dutch culture that they tried to impose. Letters and more letters were written about the great difficulties the Dutch experienced in trying to adapt. Prince Mauritius van Nassau reporting to Holland and Father Antonio Vieira to Portugal, could not ignore the social effects caused by this failure to reconcile cultures—the situation, so filled with hopelessness and powerlessness, showed the people that this misconceived idea was not going to work.

Issues related to the Church in Brazil during the Dutch period were also contentious, in that the Inquisition came to the New World, and the Prince in turn, consciously chose to ignore it. He understood that he had in his hands an instrument of social control. He calculated that he needed the *senhores de engenho*, the majority of whom were Jews. He also had to tolerate colonists of other races. Many of the churches in northeastern Brazil were built before their arrival. One of the first was perhaps that of the capuchinhos or Franciscans. "Around 1577, by invoking Nossa Senhora das Neves, Dona Maria Rosa, widow of Pedro Leitão… in 1585 donated her chapel to the Franciscans" (*Dois relatórios holandeses*, Jose Antonio Gonsalves de Mello Neto).

PADRE VIEIRA – Engraving by Lemaitre (1608-1697)

Under Nassau's strict discipline, in attempting to keep order, the Prince had in each of his cities a magistrate, a *schout*, a type of constable, who was charged with checking that all of the orders were being followed in the community. This included investigating crimes, acting as chief of police, and when the law required it, sending the prisoner to Holland.

It is impossible to understate the church's influence during the Dutch conquests in the New World.

In the beginning of its conquests in New Amsterdam, for example, the Religious Council, knowing about the land and the possibilities of trading with the Indians, sent a boat up the Manhattes River, today the North River, and instructed the conquerors o make use of the beliefs of the natives, by calling out the name of the river (which was likely sacred to them) loudly. The familiar sound made them more open-minded for negotiating.

Unlike the conquests in North America, Brazil had already been a colony of Portugal, had been populated by the Portuguese, and perhaps had had a similar experience with the natives. They were probably familiar with this process then, before the Dutch arrived, having come in contact with it during the distribution of the capitancies.

At the same time that Prince Mauritius van Nassau arrived in New Holland, van Twiller was assisting with housing developments for the colonists on the other side of the East River, in 1637, and was wisely negotiating with the natives, where more precisely, he was acquiring from the Lenape Indians in Long Island, 15,000 acres in three parcels of land, today where Brooklyn is located.

The Dutch and their descendents in North America did not have the same luck or achieve the same status as those who remained in Brazil. The same techniques were used for conquering the two cities, in the two Hemispheres (in construction, for example,

Nassau only became a Prince in 1653. Prior to this he was referred to as a Count.

they were concerned about transporting bricks and substituting them for the wooden houses around the walls of the Fort, building bridges, and providing sanitation for the city), however they were never able to set up a government structure at the level of an empire in New Amsterdam, nor did they have a Count that became a Prince, like a fairy tale....

Nassau at that time in Recife, was expanding his construction plans. The Count had brought with him Frans Post, a recorder of landscapes, who accompanied him in all battles. There are various works from this period of Prince Nassau-Siegen in Pernambuco in the museums in Holland. Besides Post, the cartographer and astronomer Gaspar Schmalkalden (author of *Diário de Viagem*, 1642-1645), the painter Albert Eckhout (who documented all the local fauna and flora), and other intellectuals and cartographers also accompanied him.

He built the Cidade Maurícia, for example, on the Antônio Vaz Island (Santo Antônio today), filling in the wetlands, building streets, palaces, and bridges, including the historic bridge named after him.

On the day this bridge was inaugurated, a toll fee was charged. Each person who participated in the inauguration festival in Recife paid a small fee. Part of the celebration included a great surprise which had been announced, and was excitedly awaited—a flying cow.

At the appointed time, there appeared, in a window of the top story of a building in the Regeneração dock, a yellow cow with long horns and a long tail made of paper filled with air (see Mario Sette, *Terra Pernambucana*). A great roar of laughter arose from the crowd. This is one of the reasons the government of the Prince in northeastern Brazil is considered to have been progressive and liberal.

COACH – Work by Crispijn van de Pas – allegory, satire of the investors in tulip bulbs, who lost fortunes in the stock market of Amsterdam, represented by the triumphant "parade car" of the Goddess Flora.

Simultaneously in Holland, in the 17th century, the phenomenon of the tulipomania was fading. The importation of this plant from Turkey was short lived. Market speculation had raised a lot of hopes, and with the collapse, the loss of jobs en masse was imminent, further destabilizing the WIC in the New World.

In 1639, slaves began to appear in New Amsterdam, and their trade was the foundation of the new economic structure. For example, one of the colonists, Jocob Stoffelsen, had slaves working in the fields and cutting wood, but it was only in 1640 when Portugal became independent from Spain that the WIC began to traffic slaves from Africa. Curiously, Edwin G. Burrows, in Gotham, contradicts the records from Brazil and Portugal, noting "slaves were subject to the same laws and judicial procedures as whites," and also regarding the manner in which the Dutch in Brazil treated the slaves. There were no laws protecting the slaves until 1888, when Princess Isabel signed the Golden Law, or Lei Áurea.

The slaves were not treated in the same manner in Brazil, where "Only the official attitude or that of one of the protestant ministers differed from that adopted by the Portuguese government and the Catholics...the Dutch attempted to keep the white and the colored populations prophylactically apart" (Tempo dos Flamengos).

Father Antônio Vieira also commented on the Dutch attitude during the occupation: "Without the Blacks there is no Pernambuco." (In Gilberto Freyre, Casa Grande e Senzala).

This was why the Quilombos dos Palmares were set up by fugitive slaves, beginning in 1638. They gathered in the mountains and continued moving around, fleeing from the moendas. They fled from their owners because they could not stand the inhuman treatment they received at the hands of the overseers and *senhores de engenho*. In this respect, under the

Dutch occupation, the situation deteriorated, due to the WIC's involvement in the transport of slaves; Nassau appointed captains to hunt down the boschnegers, as they were called.

Another interesting historical situation was the Company's struggle to maintain its stability in Amsterdam. According to Laet, "WIC's colony in North America, where the Dutch traded with the natives, was quite extensive." The price of beaver and otter pelts (1640) had increased to 68,012 florins. At that time in New Amsterdam there were no social classes, only agreements made between traders and Indians.

In New Holland, Nassau implemented the institution of the escabinos—men he had chosen to be members of the district council. The escabinos raised the general populace to a respectable class beyond the level accepted by the Portuguese at that time: "Under the Dutch rule, change occurred in the sense of leveling all within a social policy" (Fórmulas Políticas, Neme).

After reading about all these issues, Jacob called Sarah, who although surprised, always enjoyed hearing about Dutch history.

Pieter Stuyvesant finally arrived in America as its sixth governor (1646-1664). The arrival of Nassau in Brazil and of Stuyvesant in America greatly pushed forward growth. He had made his career in the WIC. He had organized in New Amsterdam, in 1644, an expedition to take over St. Martin in the Caribbean.

Arming himself with twelve ships, he went to battle against the Spanish, which ended up costing him a leg. In 1630, the WIC appointed him commerce agent in the Fernando de Noronha Islands off the coast of Pernambuco, a task he performed brilliantly. He was then nominated governor of Curaçao. His final position

(Encyclopedia of American History, *by Richard B. Morris and Jeffrey B. Morris. Harper & Row Publishers, New York, 1953,1961,1965,1970,1976).*

STUYVESANT – Pieter Stuyvesant (1592-1672), Governor General of New Amsterdam (currently New York), from 1645 to 1664. Engraving from Iconographisch Bureau, Den Haag, reproduced in the book "De geschiedenis van de WIC, pg. 86, Walburg Pers, Zutphen, 1994.

was as governor of the province of New Amsterdam, where he began his administration with great vigor, implementing sanitation in the city, passing laws, and elevating New Amsterdam to a province. He elected nine magistrates and "held down" the colony until its final crisis, from July, 1663 to April, 1664.

He began by sweeping New Amsterdam—literally cleaning the city—and ordered that a new type of architecture be used; houses, for example, could no longer have wooden chimneys. In general terms, the quality of life improved. The development of Long Island began while he was in office, in 1643. Several people became prominent at that time and were true pillars of his government, for example: Isac de Forest (a large producer of beer); Adriaen van der Donck (lawyer and author of A Description of New Netherland); Jacob Steendam (poet, author of Dem Distelvinck, in which he refers to the province as the most noble place on earth); and Hendrick Couterie (painter of the only portrait of Stuyvesant).

Soon the needs of a metropolis began to appear. A hospital was set up, and midwives arrived from Holland to serve the community that was experiencing rapid growth. Its residents also demanded schools as good as the public schools in their homeland. A postal service was set up. A dock was built on the East River, which today is Pier 17. When the Dutch government in Brazil faltered, the Company sent 300 slaves from Guinea to New Amsterdam, which bolstered the prominent local businessmen. In 1650, the population in the province was 3,500, and a decade later it had increased to 9,000. It is interesting to note that in New Amsterdam 60% of the population was Dutch, while in Brazil the colony consisted almost strictly of Portuguese, Brazilians, *Mestiços*, and *Cafusos*.

After years of disputing who possessed this territory, Holland, even with its impressive record of discovery and exploration, and its having possessed the region for quite some time, lost it to the English.

Aware of the events and decadence occurring in the WIC, Stuyvesant, who knew how things actually worked within the WIC, decided to "hang it up" when he heard about Charles II's decision, in 1644, to give the province of New Amsterdam to his brother James, the Duke of York and Albany.

The latter sent a fleet under Commander Colonel Richard Nicolls who had orders to remain in New Amsterdam until he was able to take control over it. After serious threats that Fort Amsterdam would be destroyed, Stuyvesant, in an attempt to avoid further destruction and deaths, and knowing that Colonel Nicolls and his troop were not strong enough to win this battle, decided to give up on September 8, 1664. New Amsterdam was handed over to the English government.

Stuyvesant returned to Holland to present his report to his government, however, shortly thereafter returned to New Amsterdam with his wife Judith Bayard and his family. He lived on Bowery Street and ran a business until his death in 1672.

Brazilian history during the time of the Dutch, after the Prince left, was not much different. When the Prince departed from Brazil in 1644, he left a situation that was similar to Stuyvesant's. He did not return to the colony, however, but he took everything from the region with him in his baggage, except Pernambuco itself.

John Fish, in History of American Colonies, wrote: "The Dutch were a small people who founded a great republic under great discouragement."

The Brazilian colony continued its struggle, even though it was already losing, until December, 1653. After the two battles of Guararapes, General Pedro Jaques Magalhaes and the Almirante Francisco de Brito Freyre (author of *História da Guerra Brasílica*), took over what had been New Netherlands, to govern it once again, but now in the name of the Lusitanian crown.

Sarah had been surprised by Jacob's call.

"I couldn't keep myself from calling you. I have just read some more very interesting things about the Dutch in Pernambuco, Brazil, and in New York."

"Jacob, you always surprise me. I want you to know that your calls are always welcome. I have also just finished reading a book about the history of the Dutch in the 17th century. It is a story of great immigration, of people going from Europe to the New World and vice-versa: the Dutch, the Portuguese, and the Jews who fled the Inquisition. I like researching this part of the history of my ancestors, because I always find something new."

"What is the book about? Judaism?"

"No, it's actually not about religion at all. The Jewish race was mentioned, though. I see it as historic fiction, where there are actual facts, especially concerning the fleeing of twenty three Portuguese Jews, the first to arrive in New York, in 1654."

"Who's the author?"

"An American journalist," she said. "The Jews arrived in New Amsterdam at a later date than those who went to the Southern Hemisphere, you know, but they influenced the modus vivendi in the city where Stuyvesant was governor too. It's very interesting. There were many conflicts between them, especially concerning social problems that were solved later on. You have to read it—it's the best telling of a past history I've read in the last few years."

"You don't say?" he said. "Could we meet next Friday, Sarah? You can choose the restaurant...."

"Well, I don't know. My son is arriving from Paris any time now. Maybe we could all go?"

"Is he coming on business?" Jacob asked.

"Yes, but he's also bringing his wife and my grandson, whom I haven't seen for awhile. They'll be staying for a week."

"Okay, it's up to you."

"I'll get back to you, I promise, before Friday."

After this short exchange with Sarah, Jacob decided to go for a run. His daily ritual was to go down to Riverside Park, and on the boardwalk do his first set of warm-ups, then run on to the marina facing the Palisade where he kept his boat. After jogging two miles towards North Hudson, he returned the same way and got into his boat. He loved solitude and that's where he found it. This time of the year, at the end of the first semester, he would always spend a few hours in his boat correcting his students' research papers.

The sunrise was beautiful, and the afternoon felt like the tropics.

"We'll be there within the hour," her son told her over the phone, calling from the airport.

"I'll be waiting."

She said a quick good-bye and went straight into the kitchen....

"My, you look handsome. Let me give you a kiss, Junior."

They had just arrived and were hugging each other happily.

The boy was 10 years old, very good looking, smart, blond like his grandmother, and looked like his grandfather, Sarah's father. He was already in secondary school in France. He loved to discuss politics, which should have been difficult for him to understand, and his main interest was unions, to the surprise of his grandmother.

"Grandma, I have read some of your writings about the never-ending war between the Palestinians and the Jews, and I don't understand your opinions about how it's all going to work out."

"What do you mean, Junior?"

"You wrote that you don't think that Sharon is the right person for the position, that you think he is belligerent. But I think he must be a strong person to be able to handle all the fighting around him."

"Well, that's not the only reason. He is from the most radical group in Israel (the Likud party). I think he provokes things unnecessarily. I just hope that in the January 2003 elections the labor party wins and can create the Palestinian state, and maybe bring peace, finally to Israel and the region."

"Grandma, I'd rather look at this from a religious point of view—I really think that we are approaching Armageddon."

"What's all this talk, Junior? It's a historical, religious, and geographic question; it is not an apocalyptic story. After all, that's where our sacred sites are, and the Christian's and some of the Muslim's too."

"What are our sacred sites?"

"The Wailing Wall that is west of the ruins of the ancient Temple of Solomon," she answered.

"I thought there had always been a lot of confusion over there, but the way you describe it now, Grandma, it seems to be a peaceful place."

"Well, it's not, really. You said you've read my writings. Did you understand everything?"

"Yes, Grandma."

"Then you must have read how it all happened. Our Brazilian representative to the United Nations in 1948, Oswaldo Aranha, presided over the General Assembly in New York in which the State of Israel was created.

Previously, Israel had been protected by England. Before things got better, they got worse—even after the State of Israel was created, there was a lot of confusion there."

She continued, "The population also increased tremendously, with families returning to Israel, which made life difficult there. We can talk more about this later. Dinner is almost ready. Let's go eat."

"And how are you doing, Theodelina? How is your childcare center? How many children do you have there, now?"

"It's going well, Sarah. I can now say that everything's under control. The year before last was pretty difficult, though, right after we opened, at the end of 2001. I'm not so vulnerable now, and I think the parents feel the nation is more secure. We have 47 children, Monday through Friday."

"That's good! But, I keep reading that the embassies in Paris are still being threatened."

"That's true, but under Jacques Chirac things are all right; for example, France didn't want to get involved with Bush and Blair in the hunt for Bin Laden and Saddam Hussein."

"I can see why not, Theodelina, 80% of the French are descendents of Muslims, besides the fact that France's TOTAL imports gasoline from Iraq..."

"That might be part of the reason, but I'm not sure ...all I know is that I have taken one course after another about internet safety," Ben interrupted.

"Did you come to take another one of these courses or can you stay longer with me this time?"

"Oh, Mom! I came to take another course—it's a week long and already starts on Monday."

"Well, all right. Here, you sit at the head of the table, Ben; Theo, why don't you sit to his right; Junior, on the other side, and I'll sit at this end near the kitchen. I have smoked salmon with a creamy cheese sauce, toast, biscuits, and a salad for starters. Open the wine please, Ben. I hope you like this Argentinean wine—I think it's wonderful—it's Sauvignon Blanc 1998."

"I'm sure we'll like it, Sarah. You always have good taste. Can I help you in the kitchen?"

"Yes, if you could take the plates to the table, they're all sitting out here. Would anyone like mushroom soup?"

"Junior, you can only have one glass of wine, so you can sleep tonight."

"Okay, Grandma, Okay."

"I'll have some soup, Mom."

"I'll keep you company."

"The weather is so nice here in New York. It's rained a lot in Paris. I already saw on TV that it's going to be a sunny weekend. I'd like to go for a ride around Fifth Avenue tomorrow, perhaps go to a show on Broadway."

"I recommend The Producers. I've heard it's really good."

"Mom, would you like to go with us?" Ben asked.

"Maybe. Just give me a few minutes to think about it. Would this be tomorrow?"

"Yes."

Sarah went to her bedroom to call Jacob and agreed to meet him at the door of the theater the following day, accompanied by her son and daughter-in-law. They would need four tickets then. She told him she would get back to him with more information the following day, and she returned to the table.

"Is it really good?" Theo asked.

"People say it is, but I haven't seen it yet. If you'd like, you can buy the tickets over the internet—it's faster. I have The New York Times here. Would you like to read the review?"

Sarah lived in the heart of Manhattan, midtown, on 57th Street, between First and Second Avenue. She was very active and cosmopolitan. She went to the newspaper office every day and was involved in philanthropic activities, working twice a week with one of the organizations associated with the U.N. She was sought-after as a speaker, having taught at NYU, and always attended the NYU executive and social alumni meetings.

She had opted to live alone after becoming a widow, and put all her energy into her work at The Day, the second most popular newspaper in New York after The New York Times.

She kept in touch with and visited friends she had had since her husband John was alive. They were close friends because they had raised their children together. They went out to play golf, which she really enjoyed, or just for a boat ride, which often ended up as a grand "fishing spree." She also loved to go horseback riding, and to go skiing in Vail and in Switzerland during the winter.

"I prepared a delicious steak, baked potatoes with sour cream, and your favorite vegetable, Ben."

And they both said at the same time, "Asparagus."

"Are you going to tell us your secret, Mom?"

"What secret? I don't have any secrets."

"So what's all this rush to make a phone call from the bedroom and get things ready for tomorrow?"

"Oh! I have a good friend, a professor at Columbia University—he teaches Anthropology—and we exchange information about the two Dutch colonies in the New World in the 17th century," she replied.

"That's fascinating. Is he Dutch too? What is his name?"

"Believe it or not, he is a direct descendant of Spinoza, who was also Dutch."

"Wow! I'd like to meet him. We could invite him to have dinner with us after the theater. What's his name?"

"For your information," she said, "Jacob already knows about our family in Recife and almost everything about the time of Nassau there."

"At the Olive Garden, maybe?" Ben suggested.

"All right. We'll need to get the tickets first, so I can invite him."

Theo made the phone calls while Sarah caught her son up on all the news. After all, she hadn't seen him for several months. They had a long talk about the current situation of the United States, the Republican policies of G.W.B., the grieving that hung over New York of all who couldn't bury those who had died in the tragedy of September 11, and the paranoia of all the others.

"Did you like this cabernet? It's wonderful, isn't it?"

"Now, what would you like for dessert? There's cream of papaya with cassis liquor or creme brulee, cheese, fruit, tea, coffee?"

"I love creme brulee, Grandma."

"I pass," chimed in Theo.

"Me too, Mom."

"I'll keep you company, Junior."

They had a very pleasant evening together around the table, until finally the candles burned low, and the couple was very drowsy, not able to keep the conversation going. So they retired, and Junior was already snoring lightly in the arms of Morpheus, in front of the TV in the other room.

The following morning was bright and clear.

Early in the morning, Jacob called Sarah, not waiting for her return call. He was excited about the evening, wanting to know when the show began and accepted her invitation to dine with the family.

At seven o'clock sharp, the three met Jacob in front of the theater. Ben and Theo greeted him like an old friend of the family, in a very friendly and relaxed manner. He was, after all, a very open and charming person.

Sarah, however, made it clear that he was only a friend, which was true.

The food was great and the ambience was as wonderful as usual in this restaurant chain.

The main topic of conversation was obviously the musical, which they had really enjoyed—a musical by Mel Brooks! They laughed a lot as they discussed various scenes. They talked about many other things, including the eternal saga of the Jews seeking a place in the sun.

Theodelina was telling them about an article she had just read in the Jerusalem Post about a Dutch activist, Gerda Duisenberg, who was anti-Semitic and had put up an OLP flag in front of her house, causing a lot of discomfort in her neighborhood in Amsterdam.

Ben, seeing that his wife was struck by the story, disagreed with the attitude of the activist, almost starting an argument with Theo, who had nothing to do with it.

Jacob remained neutral, simply talking about the show.

"The issue is not to debate or discuss the number of suicide terrorist attacks," Ben said, "but I think that this lunatic was just agreeing with Yasser Arafat as to the removal of the Israelites from the West Bank (Cisjordania) and the Gaza Strip!"

They discussed some fairly heavy topics, but all pretty much agreed that the nation of Israel was seeking peace.

Sarah finally started to discuss the book she had read a few days ago, which she was using to write her next newspaper review.

"Are you referring to the book that describes the two Dutch colonies in the 17th century?" Jacob asked.

"Yes. I'll lend it to you as soon as I get a few references from it. I can tell you, though, that it's very interesting. The review will come out in the Sunday issue in the second section, and I'm going to let you read it so we can discuss it."

As they were saying their good-byes, Jacob asked Sarah if she needed a ride (he had forgotten she wasn't alone). She responded by thanking him and saying she would be going home with the kids. He told her he'd call her after reading the review in the Sunday paper.

Sarah wrote the review of the book for her newspaper—Stigma, Saga for a New World.

"Even though the Jews and the nonJews are more accepting of each other in Recife, Brazil, this year, the author points out that there now exists an inversion of the religious Inquisition. She explains the concept of Stigma by showing that currently, in the 21st century, the Jews and the Christian Americans are once again being persecuted, however, this time it is by the Muslims.

"From this perpective, she introduces in the first chapter, the reason the Jews settled in Pernambuco. The book then expands the reader's view to a macrocosmic level, presenting the economic, historical, and religious situation in the New World, from the 17th century to the present.

"She avails herself of various concepts to present reasonable explanations about Brazilian culture, which is so rich.

"Beginning with an exhibit of Albert Eckhout and other Dutch painters in the 17th century, she shows the influence of Prince Mauritius de Nassau during the

Quando una sociedad llega a convencerse de que posee una verdad absoluta, cae a menudo en la tentación no de transmitir esa verdad, tendencia legitima y hasta lovable, sino de imponerla, destruyendo todo aquello que entiende que se le opone. Lo hace ademas – ai conviccion de que esta haciendo um bien. Esto sucedio en la Espana de 1492.

Dutch government in Brazil, and especially in Mauricia City where he left his mark still visible today.

"The main character makes the story flow and revolve throughout the book, reliving historic facts and interacting with the present, which occurs in the first chapter, when she brings in the exhibition in the Museum of the Indian in New York.

"In an addendum here, a pertinent statement is made in *La expulsión de los judios de España* (by Luiz Suarez), where all the exodus caused by the Inquisition began:

> *When a society has convinced itself that it possesses an absolute truth, it is tempted to not transmit this truth, a legitimate and even honorable tendency, but to impose it, destroying everything that it believes is in opposition. And it does this believing it is doing good. This occurred in Spain in 1492.*

"Within this intermezzo she has created, she presents the savage story of the first 23 Sephardic Jews who left Brazil in 1654, when the WIC was already weakening, venturing out to New Amsterdam in a continuous saga for their New World. We are then given insight into the mechanism of the West India Company, which leads us to an understanding and to the conclusion of the Stigma of this book.

"I would recommend it."

By Sarah Herckmann

New York as seen from the Hudson River

BIBLIOGRAPHY

FOR STIGMA

DE JESUS, Varela Marcos. **História Naval Brasileira, a expedição de Lopes de Hoces ao Brasil** (II vol), IA, (not dated).

DE MELLO, Evaldo Cabral. **Olinda Restaurada, guerra e açúcar no Nordeste 1630-1654**. Topbooks Editora, Rio de Janeiro, 1998.

VIEIRA, Pe. Antonio. **Papel a favor da entrega de Pernambuco aos holandeses**. Obras várias, 3 vols., Lisboa 1951, I.

DUTCH AUTHORS ON WEST INDIAN HISTORY. A Historiographical selection. The Hague -Martinus Nijhoff, 1982. Koninklijk Institut Voor Taal. Leiden, The Netherlands, 1982.

VAN DE NEDERLANDEN, Schepen. **Van de late middeleenwen tot hat einde van de 17 e eeuw.** Amsterdam, P. N., Van Kampen & Zoon N.V. – 1970.

POSTMA, Johannes Menne. **The Dutch in the Atlantic Slave Trade 1600-1815.** Cambridge Press, 1990.

DEN HEIJER, Henk. **De geschiedenis Van de WIC.** Walburg Pers, Zutphen, 1994.

ISRAEL, Jonathan. **Spain and the Dutch Sephardin, 1609-1660**. Studia Rosenthaliana, Vol XII, 1978.

DAAKU, K. Y. **Trade and politics on the gold coast 1600 to 1720**, Oxford, 1970.

ISRAEL, J.I. **The Dutch Republic and the Hispanic World, 1606-1661**. Oxford, 1982.

BOXER, C.R. **The Dutch seaborn empire, 1600-1800**. Leiden, 1967. **The Dutch on the Amazon and Negro in the seventeenth century**. English Historical review, XVII, (1903), XIX (1904).

KLOOSTER, WIM. **Illicit Riches**. Kitlv Press, Leiden, 1998.

GONSALVES DE MELLO NETO, Jose Antonio. **Dois Relatórios Holandeses**. Secretaria do Interior e Justiça, Arquivo Público Estadual. Separata da Revista do Arquivo Público. Ano IV, Nº. VI, Recife, 1949.

BEL BRAVO, Maria Antonia. **Diaspora Sefardi**. Editorial MAPFRE SA. Madrid, 1992. (ref. Biblioteca/ Joaquim Nabuco = 403/97).

CARRETE, Carlos **EI Judaismo Espanol y la Inquisicion**. Editorial Mapfre. Madrid, 1992. (ref. Joaquim Nabuco = 402/97).

18 - SALVADOR, José Gonçalves. **Cristãos-Novos, Jesuítas e Inquisição**. Editora Enio Matheus Guazzelli & Cia. Ltda. S. Paulo, SP. 1969. (ref. Joaquim Nabuco =300/200).

BRASIL-HOLANDES, DUTCH-BRASIL. Editora INDEX, Rio de Janeiro, 1995. Publicação da Petrobrás. (ref. Joaquim Nabuco = 223/98).

SUAREZ, Luis. **La Expulsão de los judios de España.** Editorial Mappfre. Madrid 1991. (ref. Joaquim Nabuco = 414/97).

SOUTHEY, Robert. **História do Brasil.** Editora Obelisco, S. P. 1965. Tradução do inglês por Dr. Luis Joaquim de Oliveira e Castro. (3ª. Ed.3º. V.). (ref. Joaquim Nabuco = 153-80, vol. 3)
(Photos pg. 41 = Mauritiopolis e Frota Bravata no Brasil).

SCHAPPES, Morris U. **A documentary History of the Jews in the United States, 1654-1875.** The Citadel Press. NY, 1950. (ref. Joaquim Nabuco = 956.94, D 637).

RODRIGUES, José Honório **Historiografia e Bibliografia do Domínio Holandês no Brasil.** Ed. D.I.N., Rio de Janeiro, 1949.

KAYSERLING, M. **Isaac Aboab, the first Jewish author in America**, in Publications of the AJHS, no. 5, 1897.

BLOOM, Herbert Ivan. **A study of brazilian jewish history 1623-1654, based chiefly upon the findings of the late Samuel Oppenheim**, in Publications of the AJHS, nº. 33, 1934.

BASSELAAR, José Van Den. **Maurício de Nassau, esse desconhecido.** FAPERJ, Rio de Janeiro, 1982. (ref. Biblioteca Nacional RJ = VI376-6-33).

PLUIS, Jan. **De Nederlands Tegel, Decors en Benamingen 1570-1930**. Nederlands Tegelmuseum, Leiden, 1977.

VAN DAM, J.D. **Nederlands Tegels**. Veen-Reflex, Ultrecht/ Antwerpen, 1988.

VAN SALBEN, Kunsto. **Antieke Tegels, Antique Tiles, Carreau Anciens**. Johan Ten Broecke, Arno Van Sablen, Richard Wondenberg. Antiquitein, Ooststraat 32 3261 Km. Oud-Beijerland, Feb. 2000.

MORTAES, José Mariz de. **Nobrega, o primeiro jesuita do Brasil**. Imprensa Nacional, RJ, 1940.

MENDONÇA, Licenciado Heitor Furtado de. **Primeira Visitação. Denunciação de Pernambuco 1593-1595**. Notas de Rodolfo Garcia. Serie Eduardo Prado. Para melhor conhecer o Brasil. Homenagem de Paulo Prado. S. Paulo, 1929.

CARNEIRO, Edison. **O Quilombo dos Palmares** Editora Civilização Brasileira S.A. (sem data).

ANTONIL, João de André. **Cultura e Opulência do Brasil, por suas drogas e minas**. Officina Real. Deslandesiana, Lisboa, 1710.

RICHSHOFFER, Ambrósio. **Diário de um soldado da Companhia das Índias Occidentais** (1629-1632). Governo do Estado de Pernambuco. Secretaria da Educação e Cultura, Recife 1977, Vol XI.

BARREIRO, José Maria Siqueira. **EL Brasil Restituido**. Obra de Lope de Vega (1625), peça teatral de Barreiro J .M. V. (Coimbra 1950) em Gente da Nação, Cristãos-novos e judeus em Pernambuco de José Antônio Gonsalves de Mello, Editora Massangana / Fundação Joaquim Nabuco, Recife, 1996.

GONSALVES DE MELLO, José Antônio. **Gente da Nação, cristãos-novos e judeus em Pernambuco 1542-1654**. Editora Massangana / Fundação Joaquim Nabuco, Recife, 1996.

FREYRE, Gilberto. **Sobrados e Mucambos, decadência do patriarcado rural e desenvolvimento do urbano** 4a. edição Editora Jose Olympio, 2 tomos, Rio de Janeiro, 1968.

Ã FENIX OU O ETERNO RETORNO: 460 anos da presença judaica em Pernambuco. Coordenação Alberto Dines, Francisco Moreno-Carvalho, Nachman Falbel; textos Alberto Dines...[et al.]. Brasília: Ministério da Cultura. Programa Monumenta, 2001.

RUTTEN, A.M.G. **Dutch transatlantic Medicine Trade in the Eighteenth Century Under The Cover of the West India Company.** Erasmus Publishing, Rotterdam, 2000.

BOUWSMA, William. **The Waning of the Renaissance, 1500-1640**: Yale University Press, New Haven, London, 2000.

BARLEUS, Gaspar. **História dos feitos recentemente praticados durante oito anos no Brasil.** Editora Itatiaia Ltda, Belo Horizonte; São Paulo, Ed. Universidade de São Paulo, 1974.

AZEVEDO, J Lúcio de. **Cartas do padre Antônio Vieira.** 3 vols., Coimbra, 1925-1928.

BOXER, C.R. **Relações raciais no Império Colonial Português, 1415-1825**. Porto, Editora Afrontamento, 1963.

LACOUTURE, J. **Os jesuítas**. 1. Os conquistadores. LPM Editores, Porto Alegre, 1994.

AVI- YONAH, Michael. **A history of the Holy Land.** The Jerusalem Publising House Ltd., Jerusalém, 1969.

DILLIARD, Maud Esther. **An Album of New Netherland.** Twayne publishers Inc., NYC 1963.

AILLAUD, J.P. CASTRIOTO LUSITANO ou HISTORIA DA GUERRA ENTRE O BRAZIL E A HOLLANDA, durante os anos 1624 a 1654. Quai Voltaire, Paris, no. 11, 1844.

CASAL, Aires de. **Corografia Brasílica**. Editora Itatiaia Ltda. Belo Horizonte, Brasil, 1976.

GONSALVES DE MELLO, José Antônio. **Tempo dos flamengos** Secretaria de Educação e Cultura, Departamento de Cultura, Estado de Pernambuco, 1978.

NEME, Mário. **Fórmulas Políticas no Brasil Holandês.** Editora da Universidade de São Paulo. S.Paulo, 1971.

SETTE, Mário. **Terra Pernambucana** Fundação de Cultura, Cidade do Recife, 1981.

BAYNE,S.G. **A Retrospective History of Lower New York**. Edited by the Seaboard National Bank, New York, 1921.

BAIGENT, Michael & LEIGH, Richard. **Inquisição.** Editora Imago, Rio de Janeiro, 2001.

BORCHERT, Till-Holger. **The Age of Van Eyck, the Mediterranean World and Early Netherlandish Paiting 1430- 1530** Published in conjuction with the exhibition, held at the Groeningemuseum, Bruges, Belgium, 2002.

RIBEMBOIM, José Alexandre. **Senhores de Engenho, judeus em Pernambuco Colonial, 1542-1654.** Editora do Autor, Recife, 2000.

What Life Was Like in Europe Golden Age, Northen Europe AD 1500-1675, by the Editors of Time-Life Books, Alexandria, Virginia (sem data, ISBN # 0-7835-5464-8).

ECKHOUT VOLTA AO BRASIL, 1644-2002. Instituto Ricardo Brennand, Conjunto cultural da Caixa, Pinacoteca do Estado de São Paulo Natiionalmuseet, Copenhagen, Denamark, 2002.

LIEDTKE, Walter, with PLOMP, Michiel C. and RUGER, Axel. **Vermeer and the Delft School**, Yale University Press, New Haven and London, 2001.

EMMANUEL, I.S. **Seventeenth Century Brazilian Jews: a critical review in american jewish archives.** Vol XIV, no 1. Cincinati, 1972.

DE SOLA, Pool, **Portraits Etched in Stone - Early Jewish Settlers, 1682-1831**. N. York: Columbia University Press, 1952.

SLUITER, Engel. **Os holandeses no Brasil antes de 1621**. Revista do Museu do Açúcar, I, Recife, 1968.

CARDOZO, JOAQUIM, **Observações em tomo da história da cidade do Recife no período holandês** Revista SPHAN, 4, 1940.

BOXER, Charles Ralpf, **The Portuguese seaborne Empire**. NY, 1969.

PEREIRA DA COSTA, F. A., **Revista do Instituto Arqueológico, Histórico e Geográfico Pernambucano**, 1967.

PEREIRA DA COSTA, F. A., **Anais Pernambucanos**, 28. Edição, 10 vol., Recife, 1983.

CASCUDO, Luis da Câmara, **Geografia do Brasil Holandês, documento e gravuras flamengas**. Editora Olympio (sem data).

LIPINER, E **Gaspar da Gama, um converso na frota de Cabral**. Rio de Janeiro, Editora Nova Fronteira, 1987. GONSALVES DE MELLO, José Antônio, **A Nação Judaica do Holandês**, Revista do Instituto Histórico e Geografico Pernambucano, Vol XL VIII, Recife, 1976.

BURROWS, Edwin G. Wallace, Mike. **Gothan a history of New York City to 1898**. Oxford University Press, NY, 1999.

SCHAPPES, Morris. **A Documentary History of the Jews in the USA 1654-1875**. Priflisles Schocken Books, NY, 1971.

DE VEGA, Lope, **A mis soledade voy**, em Blecua, José M. **Floresta de Lirica Espanõla**, Vol. I, pag 210. Editorial Gredo S.A., Madrid, 1968.

DIAS, Carlos Magalhães, Conselheiro Ernesto de Vasconcelos, Roque Carneiro. **História da Colonização Portuguesa do Brasil**, Litografia Nacional, Porto MCMXXI.

MELLO, Evaldo Cabral de. **O negócio do Brasil. Portugal, os Países Baixos e o Nordeste**. Rio de Janeiro, 1998.

MELLO, Evaldo Cabral e outros. **O Brasil e os Holandeses 1630-1654**. Organização Paulo Herkwnholf. GTM Editores LTDA, Recife, 1999.

GONSALVES de Mello Neto, João Antônio. **O Brasil que Nassau conheceu**. Recife, 1979.

SOLA POOL, David and Tomar. **An old faith in the new world**, Partait of Shearith Israel 1654-1954. Columbia University Press, New York, 1955.

About the Author

Val Beauchamp, as she like to be called, is an American of Portuguese descendant, born in Recife Brazil. A journalist (BS from Uniceub/Brasilia), she has covered Embassies and politics inside the Brazilian Congress. She has an MS in Literature from NYU, where she also taught Portuguese. Val took a graduate courses in Medieval Literature from Purdue University, where she also taught Portuguese and Spanish. An Honoray Member of the "Sociedad Nacional Hispanica" Sigma Delta PI since 1983, her biography is included in Marquis' Who's Who in the World. She presently produces programs for Cable Television.